WARHAMMER
ADVENTURES
STORIES IN AN AGE OF FANTASY

REALM QUEST

LAIR OF THE
SKAVEN

TOM HUDDLESTON

WARHAMMER ADVENTURES

First published in Great Britain in 2019 by
Warhammer Publishing,
Willow Road,
Nottingham, NG7 2WS, UK.

10 9 8 7 6 5 4 3 2 1

Produced by Games Workshop in Nottingham.
Cover illustration by Cole Marchetti.
Internal illustrations by Magnus Norén & Cole Marchetti.

ISBN 13: 978 1 78496 783 3

This is a work of fiction. All the characters and events portrayed
in this book are fictional, and any resemblance to real people or
incidents is purely coincidental.

See Warhammer Adventures on the internet at
warhammeradventures.com

Find out more about Games Workshop and the worlds of
Warhammer 40,000 and Warhammer Age of Sigmar at
games-workshop.com

Printed and bound by CPI Group (UK) Ltd, Croydon, CR0 4YY

REALM QUEST

LAIR OF THE

SKAVEN

STORIES IN AN AGE OF FANTASY

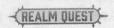

REALM QUEST

STORIES FROM THE FAR FUTURE

WARPED GALAXIES

Contents

The Mortal Realms

Each of the Mortal Realms is a
world unto itself, steeped in powerful
magic. Seemingly infinite in size,
there are endless possibilities for
discovery and adventure: floating
cities and enchanted woodlands,
noble beings and dread beasts
beyond imagination. But in every
corner of the realms, battles rage
between the armies of Order and the
forces of Chaos. This centuries-long
war must be won if the realms are to
live in peace and freedom.

PROLOGUE

Ten months ago...

The morning sun crested the peaks above the city of Lifestone, painting the rooftops, the courtyards and the crumbling towers in hazy shades of gold. Elio stood at his window gazing up towards the Arbour, the vast, tumbledown palace at the top of the hill. Its white turrets pierced the sky and its shield wall stood like a row of sentinels, watching over the city. That would be his destination, once he was done here. Once he'd decided which of his possessions he could afford to take with him, and which he was leaving behind forever.

He threw open his canvas satchel, stuffing in the weighty, leather-bound *Beastarium* that Vertigan had given him, along with a slender tome of local herblore. Around his neck he slipped a two-sided medallion bearing both the symbol of Sigmar's twin-tailed comet and the mark of the Lords of Lifestone, a silver fountain in a circle of branches. Then he opened the wardrobe and thumbed through his collection of decorative gowns – three for feast days, two for diplomatic occasions and one bright orange one that his mother had insisted would make girls notice him. He grimaced. He didn't need any of these. From now on his life would be free of formal dinners and dressing up. He was going to be a scholar.

He selected a simple white robe from the back of the closet, and took a last look around the velvet-curtained chamber that had been his study and his refuge for as long as he could remember. There was the stain on the carpet where he'd spilled a cauldron of boiled ikara root – one of his first experiments trying to brew a healing potion, and all it had done was turn his hair green. There was the Wild Birds of Lifestone chart he'd drawn himself, after months of research. The Verdian goshawk had almost taken his eye out when he got too close to its nest.

And there was the bed he'd slept in every night of his life, piled with cushions and coverlets. He wondered what would be waiting for him up at the Arbour – a nest of hay in the stables, an old stretcher in the medicus's quarters. Whatever it was, it was better than the cold barracks his father had in mind. One way or another, he had spent his last night in comfort.

He slung the satchel over his shoulder and crept to the door. The servants might wonder what he was doing wandering about at such an early hour, but they wouldn't stop him; it wasn't their place. So he stole out across the landing, tiptoeing past his father's staterooms. The family portraits seemed to frown at him as he descended the winding stairs – generation after generation of lords, glaring in disapproval at this traitor to tradition.

Elio lowered his head, crossing the pillared entrance hall with its twin shrines to the immortal King Sigmar and the Lady Alarielle. A pair of hunting dogs lay stretched by the fire, raising their heads as he passed. But the doors ahead stood wide, a pair of Freeguild guardsmen dozing in the entrance. He gripped his pack, forcing himself not to run. He was almost free.

'Son,' a voice said, and Elio's heart sank into his leather boots. His father had always been a light sleeper. Or maybe he'd suspected this would happen. The Lord of Lifestone was nobody's fool.

Elio turned, feeling his cheeks burn.

He'd rehearsed everything he was going to say if he was caught. But as he looked up into his father's stern face, his mind went completely blank.

Lord Elias strode down the steps, eyes flaming above his bristling black moustache. The silver fountain gleamed on his morning cloak, and his mouth was tight with anger.

'I'd ask where you're going, but I already know the answer. Well, you can forget it. You have a responsibility to your family and to your future, so put that bag down and return to your chambers.'

Elio almost weakened, the instinct to obey rooted deep within him. But instead he gritted his teeth, reaching inside for the strength Vertigan had assured him was there.

'No,' he said. 'Father, I'm leaving.'

'You're doing no such thing,' Elias said dismissively. He wasn't a tall man but he was a powerful one, and he would brook no insolence. 'Your place at the barracks is prepared. You will report there at midday, leaving your childish books and your childish clothes and everything else behind. You will train with the Lifestone Defenders until you come of age, just as I did, and my father, and his father. You will become a man.'

'I don't want to be a man,' Elio blurted, then realised how ridiculous that sounded. 'I mean, that's not the life for me. I don't belong in the barracks.'

'So where do you belong?' the lord sneered. 'With that crazy old man, that Shadowcaster? Learning how to sew and cook and boil up ointments?'

'Vertigan is a warrior too. He's going to teach me to defend myself.'

'Ha!' Elias snorted. 'Good luck to him!'

'I'll be his apprentice,' Elio insisted. 'I'll learn everything he has to teach.'

'Has he told you this?' Elias demanded. 'Has he said you'll be his apprentice?'

Elio frowned. 'Not in those exact

words. But he's taught me so much already. I'm going to help people, father. The way he does.'

'Who does he help?' Elias asked. 'As far as I can see he just sits in that dusty old Arbour, brooding on the way things used to be. Well, I am more concerned with the ways things are now. You were born to rule this city, Elio. Born to be a soldier and a leader of men. You will go to the barracks if I have to march you there myself.'

'I won't,' Elio insisted. 'I'm going to join Vertigan. This is *my life*.'

'No it is not!' his father bellowed, stamping his foot so hard that the floor shook. 'I brought you into this world. Your mother, Sigmar keep her, nursed you and raised you. And this great city sheltered you. You owe a debt, and you will repay it.'

'Mother wanted me to be happy,' Elio said. 'She told me I should follow my heart.'

Elias's face softened, just for a

moment. 'Do you know the last thing she said to me? Keep him safe. Whatever else you do, keep him safe. And I intend to honour that request.' He shook his head bitterly. 'Honestly, what do you think she'd say if I let you shirk your responsibilities and go off with some crazy old coot whose past is always one step from catching up to him? This Vertigan of yours has enemies, the kind of enemies you couldn't possibly conceive of.'

'What do you mean, enemies?' Elio asked, surprised. 'He never–'

'That old man's past is his business,' Elias said. 'The future of Lifestone is mine. You're my only son, Elio. What will happen when I pass on, and there's no one to take my place?'

'But I'm not saying I'll never come back,' Elio said. 'When I've learned all I can from Vertigan I'll return. Healers have been lords in the past, and scholars too. Back before... before...'

'But this isn't *before*,' Elias said,

lowering his voice so the servants couldn't hear him. Elio had seen their faces in the shadows, watching intently. 'This is now. This city is not what it was. It needs to be protected from those who wish it harm. The Lifestone Defenders have played that role for centuries, you should be proud to join their ranks.'

'Vertigan says they used to be a force to be reckoned with,' Elio told him, 'but now they couldn't fight their way out of a wool sack.'

As soon as the words left his mouth he knew he'd gone too far. He hadn't just insulted his city, but everything his father stood for. Elias's cheeks flushed and for a moment he was so angry he couldn't speak. Then he took a step back, drawing his ceremonial broadsword from its scabbard.

'You always thought you were clever,' he said. 'If you're clever enough to fight me and win, I'll let you leave. How about that?'

'I d-don't...' Elio stammered. 'I don't want to fight you, father. Anyway, I don't have a blade.'

'Give my son a sword!' Elias screamed to the guards on the door.

'But I'll lose,' Elio protested as one of them brought him a two-handed sabre. 'You're older and stronger and you've been doing this all your life.'

'Precisely,' Elias said. 'I have earned the right to be obeyed by my own son. Now take it.'

Elio was surprised by the sword's weight. He fumbled, almost dropping it.

'Hold it up,' Elias demanded. 'Come on, we don't have all day.'

'I w-won't fight you,' Elio said, starting to sob.

'Stop whimpering and swing it!' Elias barked. 'Come on, if you hate me so much, hit me.'

'I can't!' Elio screamed back. His vision was blurred, his heart racing. He saw the shadow of his father's blade and moved to block it, but he was much too slow. He felt the flat striking his backside, heard the clatter as his own sword dropped to the flagstone floor. 'Father, I'm sorry.'

'No,' Elias said. 'You don't get to call me that any more. I don't know who you are. I don't even know *what* you are. You're ungrateful, you're disrespectful, you don't care about this family or this city. You're no soldier. You're no lord. And you're certainly not my son.'

17

Elio raised his head. Elias's expression was one he knew from long experience. It was the one he'd worn when a kitchen maid stole his silver censer; the one he'd worn when two of his guards were caught drinking on duty. It was the expression he'd worn when a silk-spider had bitten him, right before he crushed it with his heel.

He waved a hand. 'Get out before I have these men arrest you, for intruding in the lord's manse.'

'F-father,' Elio managed. 'Please, d–'

'Go.' The word fell like a stone.

Elio backed to the doors, his pack heavy on his shoulder. He felt the servants' eyes on him, saw them turn one by one and slip back to their duties. The manse was silent, but through the open doorway he could hear Lifestone waking. He hung his head, and left his home forever.

CHAPTER ONE

The Light of Teclis

'Good-good man-things!' the Skaven
stammered, clutching the rune-covered
staff and retreating fearfully. 'Nice,
gentle man-things, have mercy on a
poor, pitiful Skaven, yes-yes!'

Elio stepped forwards, backing the
furry, fanged rat-creature into a corner.
'Why should we show mercy? You
showed none when you invaded our
home and tried to kill us.'

'Or when you kidnapped our master,'
Thanis added. She was covered in
bruises and her red hair was a wild
tangle. 'That's his staff you're holding.
I suggest you give it back before I

take it from you.'

Hundreds of Skaven had attacked the Arbour the night before, swarming through the palace and attacking the five children and their master, Vertigan. They'd managed to drive the creatures back, but then the Skaven leader, Kreech, had sent rats to burrow up through the floor and snatch Vertigan from right under their noses. He was dragged through a mystical gnawhole between the realms, leaving his staff behind. And now they'd caught this creature trying to sneak off with it.

The Skaven bowed, holding out the staff. Thanis snatched it. 'Now please-please,' the creature whimpered pitifully. 'Let this poor-poor vermin go.'

'Not yet,' Kiri said, holding up a hand. She was the newest member of the group, and Elio still wasn't sure he trusted her. She and Vertigan had had some kind of encounter yesterday, a run-in with a mysterious hooded lady that had left their master too weak to repel the Skaven when they attacked. Kiri claimed she couldn't remember everything that had happened.

'If you give us information,' she said to the creature, 'we'll consider letting you go.'

Its black eyes narrowed. 'What sort of information, girl-thing?'

'Where have you taken our master?' Elio asked.

'What's through that realm-hole... thing?' Thanis added.

'Who is this Kreech, and why did he come after us?' Kiri finished.

The Skaven's lips drew back over slavering fangs – it was smiling, Elio realised. 'Kreech is our packlord, servant of the Great Horned Rat and leader of the Clan Quickfang. And your master is safe-safe in our warren. You will never see his ugly man-thing face again.'

'Where is this warren?' Elio asked. 'Through the gnawhole? How many Skaven are on the other side?'

'Many thousands,' the creature grinned. Then a thought occurred and it shook its head hurriedly. 'No, few-few. Not many at all.'

Thanis threw up her steel-gloved hands. 'It's just saying whatever comes into its head.'

'Why did Kreech take our master?' Elio demanded. 'What makes him so special?'

The Skaven cackled. 'Kreech does not need me to know these things. He only needs me to fight-bite!' And it ducked its snout, shoving into Elio and trying to flee.

Elio stumbled as the creature slammed past him, baring its fangs. But Thanis swung low with Vertigan's staff, knocking the Skaven off its clawed feet and sending it tumbling across the tiled floor. It lay dazed for a moment, then it scrambled towards the door.

'Get back here,' Thanis growled, lunging forward. 'You miserable little–'

Kiri took her arm, holding her back. 'Let it go. We've got enough to worry about, and like you said it'll only tell us lies.'

Elio picked himself up, brushing off his tunic. Then he reached out to take the staff from Thanis. 'Vertigan would want me to have it,' he said. 'I was his apprentice, after all.'

Thanis's eyes narrowed. 'You were, were you?' she asked doubtfully. Then she sighed and handed it over. 'Makes no difference to me.'

They turned back to the centre of the old library, where the little inventor Alish crouched beside the sinkhole that the rats had chewed in the floor, the one they'd dragged Vertigan down into. She was studying the Light of Teclis – a gauntlet-shaped artefact crafted from black metal, with a white moonstone set into the centre. They'd learned of its existence from Vertigan's personal journal, a large, dusty tome that Alish held in her free hand. The book had

explained how powerful Skaven mystics
were able to chew holes in the fabric of
reality itself, opening gates between the
realms. The Light of Teclis could reopen
the gnawhole, allowing non-Skaven
to pass through. Or at least it was
supposed to, if only they could figure
out how it worked.

'Let me try,' Elio said, taking the
device from Alish and studying it
closely. Vertigan's book explained all
about the ratmen and how they lived,
but it said nothing about how the Light

of Teclis actually operated. Elio pointed the central moonstone down into the gnawhole and concentrated as hard as he could. Nothing happened.

'Maybe you need to say an incantation,' Thanis suggested.

'Or maybe you need to be a witch hunter to wield it,' Alish said, echoing Elio's own fears. That was the other important fact they'd learned last night – all the time they'd known him, Vertigan had secretly been a member of the Order of Azyr, an ancient society in service to Sigmar and committed to rooting out evil across the realms. Elio didn't know why the master had never taken him into his confidence – he would've kept the secret safe, even from the others. But now Vertigan was gone, and Elio didn't have the knowledge or expertise necessary to get him back.

'Or maybe it's just useless,' he said, slipping the Light from his hand. 'May as well just chuck it in the–'

'Wait,' Kiri said. 'Let me try something.'

She took the device from him, climbing down into the gnawhole. She gripped the gauntlet, then with her free hand she touched the mark on her wrist, the black rune that each of them bore a version of, even Vertigan. These birthmarks symbolised the different realms – all except for Azyr, whose power was too great for any mortal to bear.

Kiri shut her eyes, squeezing tighter. Elio felt a vibration in the air, like a whisper just beyond the limits of his hearing. The pages of the book riffled silently, then a beam of white radiance burst from the moonstone, lighting up the sides of the tunnel.

Kiri gasped in amazement. 'It's working!'

Alish grinned. 'Incredible!'

Kiri held her arm steady. 'I saw Vertigan drawing strength from his mark last night,' she said. 'So I thought maybe...'

Elio touched his own birthmark. He didn't feel any kind of power, he never had. But the marks had drawn them together, had led all five children to the Arbour, and to Vertigan. Clearly there was more to them than he'd ever suspected.

He dropped to the edge of the sinkhole, slipping in beside Kiri.

'Let me try.' Elio held the device, gripping his birthmark with his free hand. He felt a tingling beneath the skin, a sense of power radiating along his arm. The Light of Teclis seemed to tremble infinitesimally, sending vibrations up into the central moonstone. Then a pale light emerged from it, a narrow beam in which tiny motes of energy gathered and spun.

Elio crept forwards, training the Light on the end of the tunnel. He took another step, and another, and suddenly he saw that his arm had disappeared up to the wrist, now the elbow. 'Look!' he said. 'It's working! Come on, follow me!'

He started forwards but a firm hand on his shoulder stopped him.

'Wait,' Kiri said. 'We've got no idea what's on the other side. We need to think before we do anything.'

'What's to think about?' Elio demanded. 'Vertigan's through there. We need to get him back. That's all that matters.'

'But there could be a thousand Skaven on the other side,' Alish said, dropping beside Kiri. 'There could be vampires or orruks or a lake of fire, or anything else horrible that you can imagine.'

'Stay here, then,' Elio snapped. 'Stay where it's safe. But I'm going, with or without you. Vertigan gave us purpose, he made our lives mean something. He protected us, now we have to do the same for him.'

'We could use these.'

Kaspar squatted on the edge of the sinkhole, eyes bright beneath a grey hood. He had wandered off last night, right around the time they found the book. Elio wondered where he'd been, but this wasn't the time to ask.

Kaspar held up a pair of cloaks, ragged and torn at the seams. Elio recognised them – Skaven robes, presumably torn off during the fighting.

'There are all sorts of helmets and bits of armour up here as well,' Kaspar said. 'Should make decent enough disguises.'

Elio grinned. 'That's perfect. We'll sneak through and see what we can find out.'

'And what happens if they catch us?'

Alish asked. 'What happens if we're not sneaky enough?'

Thanis dropped into the hole, laying a hand on her shoulder. 'I'll look after you,' she said. 'But Elio's right, we have to go after Vertigan. He'd do it for us, wouldn't he? And besides, I've quite started to enjoy thumping Skaven. Their fur's nice and soft.'

Kiri nodded too. 'I agree. We may not know everything about Vertigan's mission and our own purpose, but we know it was important for the city, maybe for the realm. He was a soldier in the war against Chaos, and it's our time to fight too. Alish, you can always stay behind if you—'

'No,' Alish sighed, wringing her hands. 'I want to get him back as much as any of you.'

Kaspar put a hand on her shoulder. 'I'm scared too. Like, *really* scared. But as long as we're together I think we'll be okay.'

Alish placed her hand on his, and

seemed to take strength from it. She nodded firmly.

'We're agreed then,' Elio said. 'Let's round up some disguises. Oh and it's going to be dark down there – maybe we should think about bringing a tinderbox of some kind.'

At this, Alish's eyes flashed. 'You know, I think I've got just the thing.'

CHAPTER TWO

Into the Dark

Elio wrapped the stinking Skaven
robe around his shoulders and raised
the hood to hide his eyes. Under the
cloak he wore a small satchel crammed
with healing supplies and a few strips
of dried meat. He had gone through
Vertigan's notes on the Skaven again,
memorising as much as he could. This
was unlike anything he'd ever done
before, walking straight into the mouth
of danger. But he felt as prepared as
he could possibly be.

The others huddled behind him in
the tunnel, strapping on ragged bits
of boiled leather armour and wrapping

foul rags around their faces. The disguises might not stand up to close inspection – none of them had fur or fangs – but hopefully they'd blend in.

'I'm going through,' he said, tucking Vertigan's staff under his arm and holding up the Light of Teclis. The device was awake, its pale beam reflected in their fearful, excited eyes. 'If I start shouting or flying about, pull me back.'

Thanis nodded and Elio reached out, finding the place where the Light vanished into the soil. He took a deep breath and stepped forwards.

At first he could see nothing. The air was warm and close, and there was a foul, mulchy smell. But there was ground under his feet – hard earth, packed down. He shone the Light around, illuminating two walls and a low ceiling. He was in another tunnel.

He turned the beam back to the wall he'd just stepped through. Thanis's gloves appeared first, then her cautious

34

face, then her armoured torso. The others emerged one by one, staying close to the wall and to each other. Elio looked up and down the tunnel, but the shadows were deep in both directions. And as he stepped away from the gnawhole the Light of Teclis flickered out too, plunging them into darkness.

'It must only work where the realm energy is strong,' he said as he slipped the device back into his pocket. 'We shouldn't carry a light, anyway – Vertigan's journal said that the Skaven can see in the dark, they'd know right away that we couldn't.'

'So which way?' Kiri asked. 'Elio, you're the leader, you decide.'

'I'm not the leader,' Elio said. 'Am I?'

'Someone needs to be,' Kiri said. 'This was your plan, you should probably take charge.'

Elio felt his cheeks flush, and was glad she couldn't see him. But perhaps Kiri was right – someone needed to make the decisions, and he might be the best suited. He'd known Vertigan longest, and he was a lord's son too, trained in the ruling arts.

He took a deep breath. 'That way,' he said, gesturing. 'I think I felt a breeze.'

'Um, we can't actually see you,' Alish pointed out.

Elio blushed again. 'Of course. Sorry. How about I go first, Alish can hang on to me, Thanis to her, and so on. We'll go in a line.'

'Sounds good, boss,' Kaspar said, a hint of sarcasm in his voice. *Let him smirk,* Elio thought. He wouldn't be laughing when they tracked down Vertigan and brought him home.

Elio moved along the tunnel, his hands held out in front of him. He could feel warm air flowing towards them, carrying with it a musty stench of rot and rat droppings. He felt sure they were heading the right way – towards the heart of the warren, not away from it.

Then Alish squealed and let go of his

cloak, and for the briefest moment he was alone in the dark. His feeling of certainty fell away. What if something had grabbed her, what would he do then?

He jumped as she returned to his side, pressing something into his hand.

'This was on the floor. I think it's a glove.'

Elio squeezed the object between his fingers, hearing the creak of soft leather. He put it to his nose, inhaling the scent of pipe smoke. 'It's Vertigan's.'

'Could he have dropped it on purpose?' Kiri asked. 'Left it for us to find?'

Elio felt his hopes rise. 'Yes, I'm sure that's what happened. He knew we'd come after him.'

Thanis took the glove. 'So at least we're going the right w–'

'Hush,' Kaspar broke in suddenly. 'I heard something. Behind us in the tunnel.'

Elio listened for a moment, but all he could hear was his own blood pulsing.

For a moment he felt his wrist tingling, as though his birthmark was waking. *It must be because we're all here together,* he thought.

'What did it sound like?' he asked Kaspar. 'Is someone following us?'

'Or some*thing*,' Thanis muttered.

'I don't know,' Kaspar admitted. 'It sounded like footsteps, then it just stopped. Hang on, I can hear something else, though. The other way. Coming towards us.'

Elio looked around, feeling closed in. Had the Skaven found them already?

'I think the wall's shaking,' Alish said. 'What's happening?'

Elio put a hand out. He could feel the vibrations, growing stronger. He could hear the noise, too – an irregular thud up ahead. Whatever was coming it was much heavier than a man, let alone a scurrying Skaven.

'Everybody, hit the wall!' Kiri hissed. Elio threw himself back, Alish's hand grasping his. The floor trembled as something charged towards them, galloping along the narrow passage. It passed just inches from Elio's face – he smelled earth and damp fur, and somehow the darkness became even darker. Then it was gone.

'After him, Krat!' a shrill voice shrieked, and Elio lowered his hood as more footsteps hurried past, a pair of ratmen pursuing the first creature.

'Trap it, Scowlish!' the second Skaven screamed as they sprinted past. 'Don't let it go, yes-yes!'

There was a crash and a cry of surprise, then the noises faded.

'What *was* that thing?' Thanis asked breathlessly.

'I don't know,' Elio admitted. 'But it was big. And fast.'

'The disguises worked, at least,' Kaspar said. 'The Skaven didn't even slow down.'

'Well they were sort of distracted,' Kiri pointed out.

They moved on, following the flow

of warm air. Elio could feel passages opening on either side and wondered how big this warren was – according to Vertigan's book some of them could contain thousands of miles of tunnels, excavated over centuries. If they lost their way they could die of thirst before the ratmen even found them.

No, he told himself. Thinking like that wouldn't help. They'd come this far, they'd even found Vertigan's glove; he couldn't believe they would fail. True, he had no idea where their master was or how to free him. But he'd take each challenge as it came, and conquer them one by one. He was the son of a great family, he reminded himself, descended from a long line of noble lords. He could do this.

Then the tunnel opened out, and his jaw dropped in amazement.

The cave ahead of them was large enough to swallow the city of Lifestone three times over. Jagged black walls rose like mountain slopes, meeting far above their heads to form an arched roof studded with stalactites the size of temple spires. In the very centre a huge crystal structure jutted down from the rock, emitting a pale, pulsating light that illuminated the entire cavern.

Below it was another natural structure, a black mirror image of the white crystal. It rose from the cavern floor, a monolith of volcanic rock with high, sheer sides. At the base was a series of boreholes, circular openings leading down into the earth. But they

weren't what drew Elio's eye.

Because on the black pillar's flat, plateaued peak a building had been constructed – a huge, untidy edifice of stone and wood. For a moment it reminded him of the Arbour, a crumbling pile with sprawling wings and ramshackle turrets. But this was almost a mockery of that noble palace, a rickety sprawl balanced on the spire like a crow's nest in the top of a tree.

It was ringed with glowing braziers, casting a sickly green light into the cavern. Between them Elio could see figures moving, the emerald light reflected from their bronze armour.

'That's where Vertigan is,' he said. 'That's where they're keeping him. I know it.'

Kiri looked uncertain. 'How?'

Elio pointed. 'That green glow is warpstone, a sort of magical crystal that the Skaven are obsessed with. I read about it in the journal – it's like gold is for humans, a symbol of their wealth. But it gives them real power, too. It has all these unpredictable mystic properties. So that building must be where their packlord sits, this Kreech. It's where he'd take Vertigan, it stands to reason.'

'I believe you,' Alish said. 'But how are we meant to get past *them*?' She gestured downwards, and Elio felt his hopes plunge.

Ever since they'd emerged from the tunnel he'd been aware of a noise in his ears, a low roar like a distant storm. Now he realised it was the sound of thousands upon thousands of Skaven, all chattering at once. The floor of the cave was boiling with them, a teeming mass of furry, verminous life. They clambered over one another, swarming between mounds of soil where the ground had been tunnelled to make nests and burrows, scurrying through structures of wood and stone. He saw forges and factories spitting fire and smoke, machines and scaffolds where

the ratmen were working to enlarge the
cave.

'These disguises won't be any use
down there,' Alish said. 'We'll be too
close, right, Kaspar?'

She turned, and Elio saw her face
fall. Spinning around he realised
Kaspar was no longer with them – he'd
simply vanished.

'Where's he gone now?' Elio asked,
exasperated. 'Honestly, you take your
eye off him for two minutes and he
just–'

'Stop!' a cry sounded, back along the
tunnel. 'Get back!'

Kiri drew her catapult and Thanis
raised her gloves, marching back into
the dark. Elio gripped Vertigan's staff,
his heart thundering. In the dark he
could hear the sounds of a scuffle –
Kaspar cursing angrily, and someone or
something else growling like a beast.

'Can anyone see him?' he asked.
'Kaspar, where are you?'

'Hang on,' Alish said, rifling in her

pockets. 'Let me just–'

There was a sudden flash of white, lighting up the tunnel. In its glare Elio saw Thanis and Kiri storming forwards, and just beyond them Kaspar against the wall, grappling with a small, struggling shape, too little even for a Skaven. Then the light was gone.

'What was that?' Elio asked. 'That flash?'

'They're flares. Vertigan helped me make them,' Alish explained. 'I call them Bolts of Azyr.'

'Well, do another,' Elio said. 'Quick.'

This time he saw Kaspar's opponent more clearly: wide, staring eyes over a pale, filthy face.

'Thanis, help me!' Kaspar cried, wrestling the figure back towards the light. 'He's getting loose!'

She stormed in and together they laid hold of the struggling form, hauling it along the tunnel. Elio heard cries and whimpers, and heard feet scrabbling on the dry earthen floor.

Then the tunnel opened and the light grew, and he found himself staring in disbelief. The figure wore a tunic of reddish-brown cloth. Green eyes stared from beneath a mop of mousy hair, and Elio saw marks on its cheek, like whiskers drawn with mud or paint. But this was no Skaven, or any other kind of beast. There in the tunnel, baring his teeth and growling at them, stood a ragged human boy.

CHAPTER THREE

The Lost Boy

'I heard him sneaking about in the tunnels,' Kaspar said as he let the boy down. 'I think he was following us.'

The child crouched, glaring. His feet were bare and there were bruises covering his legs and arms. Alish took a step forwards and he snarled, showing his teeth like a cornered hound.

'We're friends,' she said soothingly. 'Friends. I promise.'

The boy inched away from her, then he saw Thanis behind him and moved forwards again.

'What's he doing down here?' Kiri asked.

'The Skaven could've stolen him on one of their raids,' Thanis suggested.

'Or maybe he got lost in the caves,' Kaspar said. 'Just kept wandering until he ended up here.'

'But where is *here*?' Elio asked. 'According to Vertigan's book Skaven warrens don't occupy normal space. We might not be in an actual realm, as we understand it.'

Thanis shuddered. 'That's creepy.'

'He's so thin,' Alish said, inspecting the boy's bony frame. 'We can't just leave him down here, can we? We should take him home with us.'

Elio dug in his pack, pulling out a strip of dried meat. 'We came to rescue Vertigan, not some kid,' he said, holding it out. 'We don't have time for distractions.'

The boy sniffed uncertainly, but Elio nodded and he reached out a cautious hand, ready to snatch it back if this turned out to be a trick.

Kiri gasped. 'Look! His wrist!'

They leaned closer, but somehow Elio already knew what he'd see. There on the ragged boy's wrist was a black mark – a rune like an arrow with twin shafts. The boy snatched the meat from Elio's hand then he jumped back, scoffing it loudly.

'You're one of us,' Thanis said, holding out her arm. 'You've got the mark.'

The boy stared at her, looking from her wrist to his. One by one they each exposed their marks and the boy frowned, scratching his head with long, dirty fingernails.

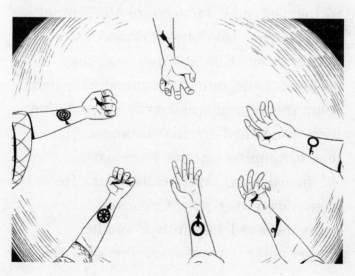

'It's the seventh mark,' Kiri said softly. 'The one Vertigan's been searching for.'

'Now we definitely have to take him back,' Alish said. 'Don't we?'

Elio nodded. Then he held up both hands and stepped towards the boy, giving what he hoped was a reassuring smile. 'You need to come with us,' he said. 'Just be calm and– Thanis, grab him!'

Startled, she reached for the boy's arm. But he was too quick, jerking back with a hiss and slamming into Alish, knocking her down. He scrambled to his feet and darted into the tunnel, disappearing into the darkness.

'After him!' Elio shouted and they sprinted back into the tunnel. The light from the cavern quickly faded and they were consumed by the darkness, their feet drumming on the hard earth.

'I heard him,' Alish called out. 'He went down this way. Come on!'

Elio followed her into a smaller tunnel, then an even smaller one, the ceiling scraping the top of his head. He tried to make a mental note of how many turns they took and in which direction, but it was hard to keep track. He felt his pulse quicken, unable to shake the feeling that they were getting deeper and deeper into danger, the kind he wouldn't be able to lead them out of.

'Where'd he go?' Alish's voice was close, startling him. 'I nearly had him then he just vanished.'

They stepped into a round chamber with thin shafts of light filtering through cracks in the ceiling, from a crystal buried in the rock overhead. There were six tunnels branching off; some were arched passages, others just clawed-out burrows.

The others joined them, skidding to a stop. 'Which way now?' Kiri asked.

Alish shook her head. 'I lost him. He could have gone down any of these.'

'Stop talking for a moment,' Kaspar said. 'Let me listen. I hear... yes, I hear something.'

'The boy?' Thanis asked.

Kaspar shook his head slowly. 'No, something bigger. It's coming towards us. I think it's the same thing as before, the thing the Skaven were chasing. We need to get out of sight.'

In the mouth of one of the larger tunnels Elio could see a green glow, bouncing from the walls. He heard the thunder of footsteps, and beneath it the cry of the Skaven. He looked around desperately. All of the tunnels looked the same.

Then there was a loud, insistent hiss, and Elio twisted round. There in the entrance to one of the tunnels crouched the ragged boy, beckoning fiercely.

'Come on,' Alish said. 'He wants us to follow him.'

They hurried into the low tunnel, crouching down and peering cautiously through the entrance as the footsteps drew closer, the green glow filling the chamber.

It came from a warpstone torch, held aloft by a running Skaven. His eyes were wide with panic as he burst into the open, skidding to a halt. His fur was black but for a grey stripe down the centre of his head, and he was breathing hard. The crash of feet was loud behind him, making the ground and the walls shake.

Then a huge black shape burst from the tunnel, roaring like something from a nightmare. It was covered all over in dense fur, with curved white claws as big as broadswords. The tip of its snout was twitching and hideous, a star-shaped knot of tentacles sniffing the air. Elio felt a

flicker of recognition, remembering the *Beastarium* that Vertigan had given him. He was sure he recognised this creature.

The Skaven whipped a sack from his belt, covering up the warpstone torch. The beast stopped in its tracks, snorting with confusion. For the first time Elio noticed that there was something on its back – the second Skaven, clinging on desperately with both hands. He wore a brown cloak and his tail was little more than a stump, wagging like a finger in the air.

The black monster pawed the ground, digging furrows with its mighty claws. Its nose writhed like an enraged kraken as it advanced on the first Skaven, dipping its head and preparing to charge. But the figure on its back was already moving, slipping down between the creature's eyes, grasping something in both hands. It was a net made of leather straps, unfolding as he flung it outwards.

There were metal loops on all four corners, weighing the net down. It dropped over the creature's snout and the second Skaven ran in, pulling the muzzle tight over that sensitive pink nose. The beast froze instantly, its eyes wide and fearful. The ratmen slung ropes through the net, tying it to a collar around the creature's neck. So they'd already caught it once and it had escaped, Elio realised. Somehow, the thought gave him hope.

The creature sank to its knees, completely docile now. The stump-tailed Skaven dealt it a sharp kick but the beast barely responded, blinking and cowering.

'Leave it, Krat,' grey-stripe said. 'These creatures are dumb-dumb, they never learn.'

'We better get moving, Scowlish,' said stump-tail. 'If we don't get those pelts to the packlord there'll be trouble, yes-yes.'

They forced the beast to its feet,

prodding and shoving it back into the tunnel. The ground shook as the creature lumbered away, then they were gone.

'Did you hear what they said?' Elio whispered as they crouched in the alcove. 'Something about the packlord. If we follow them they'll lead us to Kreech.'

'And what about our new friend?' Kiri asked. 'Maybe we should make sure he's safe at the Arbour before we...' She trailed off, looking around. Elio followed her gaze, but the boy was gone.

Alish started down the tunnel. 'Come on, we have to get him back.'

'Wait,' Elio said. 'We've got a lead on Kreech, and if we find him we find Vertigan. We have to follow those two Skaven.'

'But that boy saved us,' Alish insisted. 'He's the seventh mark. Vertigan would want us to get him back.'

Elio frowned. She had a point. 'Okay,

we'll split up. Alish, go after the boy. Thanis, go with her. Me, Kaspar and Kiri can follow those Skaven and hope they lead us to Vertigan.'

Kiri frowned. 'Are you sure that's a good idea? This is a big place, we don't know if...'

But Alish was already hurrying off into the tunnel, throwing a glance back over her shoulder. 'He can't have gone far. We'll find him and meet you back at the gnawhole.'

She vanished into the dark, and Thanis squeezed Kiri's shoulder. 'Don't worry,' she said. 'I'll keep her safe.'

Then they were gone.

58

CHAPTER FOUR

The Cart

Elio, Kaspar and Kiri crept along the
tunnel, following the bickering ratmen
and their giant captive. The floor sloped
down and there was an acrid smell,
like rotten meat and animal waste.
The light grew and soon the tunnel
opened out into the vast central cavern,
the walls rising steep and black on
either side. Elio could hear that sound
again, the busy chattering of countless
Skaven. He could see the tower of rock
in the heart of the cave, topped with
that strange wooden structure. *Hold on,
Vertigan*, he thought. *We're coming.*

They crouched in the tunnel's

mouth, watching as the Skaven led
the docile beast down a short slope
to a wooden paddock, opening a gate
and driving it inside. In the paddock
Elio could see more of the creatures,
lowing and grumbling like a herd
of huge cattle. One of them moved
towards the newcomer, dropping its
head and rubbing a muzzled snout
against its side. There was something
affectionate about it, and suddenly Elio
remembered.

'Delvers mate for life,' he said,
recalling a passage from his beast book.
'That's what they're called. Deepearth
Delvers. Though in some realms they
name them Burrowing Blackpelts.
They're ferocious when cornered,
but otherwise placid. And they love
warpstone, as we saw.'

Kiri shook her head in amazement.
'How do you remember all this stuff?'

Elio blushed. 'I just like learning
about different creatures. It's
interesting.'

'Look at that,' Kaspar said, gesturing. 'I wonder what that place is for.'

The Skaven had crossed an open courtyard beside the paddock, entering a large wooden shack. The iron door banged behind them.

'We have to get closer,' Elio said. 'Do you really think the disguises will work?'

'It's all about confidence,' Kaspar said. 'That's the trick to sneaking around, you need to look like you know where you're going. The disguises are good, but try to move like a Skaven, all quick and shifty. Keep your arms sort of hunched up under your chest and keep your head low, like this.'

Elio gave it a try, scuttling forwards with his head down. Kiri followed suit, and Kaspar nodded encouragingly. 'You're both a bit tall, but I think you'll pass.'

They scurried forwards, circling through the shadows towards the hut. Elio tried to make every movement as twitchy as possible, feeling slightly ridiculous as he bowed his legs and narrowed his shoulders. But then a band of Skaven passed a short distance away, making for the tunnel, and barely even glanced their way. Elio felt his confidence grow. It was working.

They reached the shack, pressing against the rickety wooden wall. There was a window set into it, and Kiri craned up to peer through. Her mouth turned down in disgust.

'What are they doing?' Elio asked. 'Cutting up meat?'

Kiri shook her head. 'They're drying skins. Delver skins. They must keep them for the fur.'

Elio frowned. 'I really hate those Skaven.'

Between the wall of the shack and the side of the cave was just enough space for them to squeeze through. They crept alongside, foul smells leaking from the shack. Peering around, Elio saw that a ramp led down from the shack and at its base was a wooden table.

Beside the table stood the largest Skaven Elio had seen so far. He wasn't tall or muscular, he was just very fat, his leather waistcoat stretched over a round, brown belly. He wore a red felt hat, tipped back on his oversized head.

'Hey, I've seen him before,' Kiri whispered, looking over Elio's shoulder. 'Back at the theatre. He was with Kreech – he's his assistant or something.'

The door to the shack swung open and the first two Skaven emerged, their arms heaped with black furry objects. 'Many-many apologies, oh great Major-Domo Lesh,' said stump-tailed Krat as he deposited the skins on the table. 'We had some trouble with one of the beasts, yes-yes.'

'Not good enough, foul-foul Krat,' the big Skaven rumbled. 'Or you, feeble Scowlish. You keep the master wait-waiting, yes you do.'

Scowlish bowed too, pressing his clawed hands together. 'Forgive, oh Lesh. Admire the fine-fine skins.'

The fat Skaven snatched the nearest pelt, stroking the black fur appreciatively. 'These will do,' he said, reaching into a pouch and pulling out a glowing crystal. It looked like warpstone, Elio thought, but instead of the usual green this was a deep, rich violet colour. Krat received it gratefully, bowing almost to the floor.

'I think-wonder,' the large Skaven

asked, 'have you seen the master's pet? Lord Kreech has been wondering where he might have escaped to. He cares so for the little scrapling.'

Scowlish bowed again. 'We smelled it,' he said. 'Didn't we, Krat? A foul stench, up in one of the tunnels.' He gestured back the way they'd come.

Lesh frowned. 'I'll send a search party. Fool-fool creature, always scurrying away.' He looked down at the skins. 'Have these loaded into the rail-cart and brought to the packlord's chambers, quick-quick. You can pay for your tardiness by pulling the wagon yourself.'

He marched away into the cave leaving Krat and Scowlish staring after him, their expressions somewhere between hurt and anger.

'Pull it ourselves,' Krat muttered, his stump of a tail bobbing furiously. 'I told you that disgusting delver would cause us trouble, Scowlish.'

Scowlish snarled. 'It shall pay, though,

oh Krat. We shall take its skin,
yes-yes.'

They gathered up the pelts, carrying
them to a wooden cart on the far side
of the yard. It had large metal wheels,
resting on steel rails. They dropped the
pelts inside then retreated to the shack,
the door slamming behind them.

'Quick,' Elio said, slipping out of
hiding. 'Let's go.'

'Where?' Kiri asked, looking around.

Elio gestured to the cart. 'You heard
him. They're taking the delver pelts
to Kreech. This is our chance to find
Vertigan.'

He ran to the cart, the others close
behind him. Elio lifted one of the
pelts, wrapping it around his shoulders.
It was huge, enveloping his entire
body. Then he climbed into the cart,
pulling the skin over his head. Kaspar
clambered in, burying himself up to the
neck, and Kiri squeezed in beside him,
crouching in the pile of furs.

'Of all the crazy things we've done

today,' she said, 'this is by several leagues the craziest.'

'And another terrific smell,' Kaspar muttered.

'It'll work,' Elio whispered. 'Trust me.'

He heard Krat and Scowlish returning, grumbling bitterly. Elio raised his head cautiously to see them strapping a leather harness around their shoulders, and hooking it to the cart.

'Ready-ready,' Krat rasped. 'One, two-two, three!'

They strained on the ropes and the cart ground forwards, wheels screeching. The rails were bolted to wooden sleepers, lifting them off the rocky, uneven floor. The axles creaked as the Skaven pulled, dragging the cart to the top of a shallow incline, cursing with every step. Then they rolled over the top and down the other side, Krat and Scowlish forced into a jog as the cart picked up speed.

'Quick-quick,' Scowlish squealed. 'The pelts are heavy today.'

'Fine-fine craftsmanship is always more weighty,' said Krat knowledgeably.

Elio peered out as the wagon rolled through the sprawling warren. On either side were mounds of soil and dark holes leading down into the earth. Skaven swarmed everywhere – he saw warriors in leather and copper; slaverats dragging barrows piled with earth, metal and meat; priests with their smoking censers, chanting prayers to the Great Horned Rat.

The rails rose onto an elevated wooden scaffold high above the floor of the cave, and a few Skaven peered up as they rattled overhead. Elio saw one of them shaking his head, obviously not convinced by this new-fangled technology.

Then the cart slowed, and he ducked lower as they drew to a halt beside a rickety platform built from timber and planks. A group of Skaven climbed onto the tracks, tying a second carriage to the first. It was heaped with crates and bottles, clinking and rattling as Krat and Scowlish put their heads down and began to pull again, straining with the increased weight. The second group of ratmen watched, cackling gleefully. The carts rolled deeper into the cavern.

'I wish Alish could've seen this,' Kiri whispered. 'She'd have loved this contraption.'

Elio frowned. 'I hope they're okay. Maybe we shouldn't have let them run off like that.'

'It was the right thing to do,' Kaspar assured him. 'It's like Alish said, that kid with the seventh mark is important. Anyway, Thanis'll keep her safe. She's tougher than she looks.'

Elio squinted at him. 'But she looks really tough.'

Kaspar grinned. 'Exactly.'

There was a clunk and the cart came to a sudden halt. Peering up Elio saw Krat and Scowlish unstrapping their harnesses with groans of relief. Had they reached their destination? Behind them the warren sprawled, murky in the base of the cavern. To one side was a rugged cliff of black stone – the wall of the cave? No, he realised, it was the spire in the centre, stretching up and out of sight. Far above he could see a white glow tinged with green. The tracks kept going, turning along the side of the cliff and rising out of sight. So why had they stopped?

Krat crouched on the tracks, his stump twitching as he fumbled with some sort of mechanism. He stepped back, nodding to Scowlish, who tugged on a large wooden lever. With a jerk, the cart started forwards again. But now there was no one pulling.

Elio leaned over the front. Between the rails was a chain made from interlocking steel segments, locking into cogs on the cart and hauling them uphill.

'Ingenious,' Kaspar said.

Kiri pursed her lips. 'We could've used one of these in the slave camp, for lifting rocks. Rather than forcing people to do it.' For a moment her eyes were far away and Elio knew she was seeing the place in her memory, reliving the horrors she'd witnessed. Slavery had taken her mother's life, and Kiri herself had barely escaped.

The incline grew steeper, the cogs clicking as they ground jerkily up the face of the cliff. 'I guess we're going all the way up there,' Elio said uncertainly, gazing at the rickety manse high above.

'I think so,' Kaspar agreed. 'The best thing is not to look down.'

But Elio couldn't resist. He peered over the edge, and the view made his head spin. The tracks were fixed to beams bolted to the cliff; below them was nothing but empty air. The cavern floor was already far beneath them, the chain dragging them link by link up the wall of rock. Elio ducked back, a little too quickly. The cart shuddered ominously.

'I think we should try not to move

about too much,' Kaspar said. 'These wagons aren't exactly stable, and we *really* don't want to go over the edge.'

CHAPTER FIVE

The Barracks-Nest

Up and up the carts climbed, hugging
the side of the cliff. In several places
the track divided, with branch lines
running horizontally along the rock
face, supported by lengths of rickety
scaffold. But the main track kept
ascending, the chain beneath them
clanking and protesting.

Suddenly the sound changed, and
looking down Elio saw that they were
rolling over solid rock, the rails bolted
to a level outcropping halfway up the
rock face. The chain vanished into a
hole in the cliff and the rails sloped
briefly downhill, sending the cart

around a sharp bend until it latched on to a new chain on the far side. Then they were rising again, switching back across the face of the precipice.

Looking up he could see the mansion clinging to the peak high above them. It was built on iron stanchions hammered into the rock, supporting the weight of the main structure. It was sort of impressive in its way, presiding proudly over the cavern. If only it didn't look like it was ready to fall apart at any moment. It reminded Elio of a child's drawing, a half-finished scrawl of a place.

They rattled through another bend and into the final stretch, passing beneath the ring of warpstone braziers on the slopes below the peak. Beside each one stood a pair of armoured Skaven, facing out into the cave. Elio wondered what they were supposed to be guarding against, all the way down here. Or perhaps they were just for show, to make Kreech feel powerful.

'What's the plan when we get up there?' Kiri whispered.

Elio shrugged. 'Find Vertigan. Don't let them catch us.'

She smiled. 'Simple but effective.'

There was a clunk and they were back on the flat, the cart trundling along the exterior edge of a wooden outbuilding that clung to the rock. The tracks dipped and they slid smoothly through an opening in the side, clunking to a stop.

They were in a storeroom, piled with crates and delver skins. Pale light slanted through gaps in the ceiling from the massive crystal overhead. Elio slipped the pelt off his shoulders, ready to climb out. Then a door creaked and he heard voices, and dropped back into the cart.

'It's here, yes-yes!' It was Kreech, his oily tones horribly familiar from the fight in the Atheneum. 'Wasn't this a clever-clever invention of mine, oh faithful Major-Domo Lesh? Delivering all these goodies right to my store-door.'

'You are wise-wise, oh Kreech,' another voice said, and Elio matched it to the large Skaven they'd seen back at the delver farm. He sounded out of breath, as though he'd run all this way. 'Your rail-cart is truly a miracle. So much more quick-quick than the one we saw in the Blightwarren last year, yes-yes.'

Kreech gave a snort. 'I do not remember that. If another warren has a similar invention they must have stolen it from Kreech. Now stop this talk-talk and show me your wares, foolish Lesh.'

Elio heard the boards creak as they came closer. 'Look, more beautiful furs,' Lesh said. 'So silky-soft, so black-black. And here, wine and meat from the raiders, so generous of them, yes-yes.'

'Not generous,' Kreech snarled. 'I am their packlord and ruler. I, Kreech. It is my right.'

'Yes-yes,' Lesh agreed. 'You should demand more-more. Another cart load. For their insolence.'

Kreech sniffed. 'See that it is done. Now, I must return to my prize. Have these furs brought to my chamber for inspection. I do hope that this time the fleas have been properly pick-picked.'

'Yes, mighty Kreech,' Lesh said, licking his lips. 'I will see to it personally.'

Elio peered out as they strode away, through a large set of wooden doors on the far side of the loading dock. Then he climbed carefully from the cart onto the platform, followed by the others.

'Did you hear that?' Elio whispered. 'My prize. He must mean Vertigan.'

Kaspar frowned. 'That's quite a big leap, isn't it? He could've meant anything, gold or furs or–'

'We don't know what he meant,' Kiri said. 'But it's worth looking into.'

They crossed to the door and Kiri inched it open cautiously. Inside all was darkness, but they could hear a strange, deep thrumming sound.

'What is that?' Elio whispered. 'A machine of some sort?'

He prepared to step inside, but froze when he heard a sudden hiss from behind them. The ragged boy crouched beside a stack of crates, peering at them beneath his cloth hood. There were ears stitched into it, Elio noticed – a clever way to make himself look like a Skaven. The boy pointed to the door and shook his head insistently, making claws with his hands and baring his teeth.

'I think he's saying there are Skaven in there,' Elio said.

'What's he doing up here?' Kaspar asked dubiously. 'And where are Alish and Thanis?'

Elio crossed towards the boy. 'Have you seen our friends?' he asked, miming two figures, one tall and one short. But the boy just stared back dumbly, his eyes glittering in the pale light.

'Or our master,' Kiri said, joining Elio. She mimed a beard, then pretended to smoke a pipe. This time the boy's eyes lit up and he nodded vigorously.

'You have?' Elio asked. 'Where? Take us to him.'

The boy grinned, pointing to a window high overhead. Then he clambered onto the stack of crates, leapt aside to land on a rickety shelf, and grabbed hold of the window to pull himself up. He paused on the ledge, beckoning.

Kaspar looked up doubtfully. 'We don't know where this kid came from.'

'But he's one of us,' Elio argued. 'He's got the mark.'

'That doesn't mean he's on our side. Not everyone's as trustworthy as you, Elio.'

'He helped us before,' Kiri pointed out. 'And if he can lead us to Vertigan...'

Kaspar nodded. 'I know. I just think we should be cautious.'

Elio hauled himself up, hopping from stack to stack the way the boy had done. The shelf groaned beneath him but he managed to reach the window, following the boy out onto a steep, exposed roof. Above their heads the crystal gleamed like a fractured sun, and on either side was a sheer drop, down the cliff to the warren below. He gulped and scrambled up.

They came to a second opening, this one leading into a larger outbuilding attached to the main structure. Inside Elio could see only blackness. The boy squirmed through, nodding and gesturing. Elio glanced back, seeing Kiri and Kaspar crawling up the steep roof. Then he followed.

Inside it was warm and dark, a little light leaking through the slatted roof. There was a foul smell and the air was filled with that strange rumbling, thrumming sound.

'What is this place?' Kiri whispered, following Elio through. The ragged boy glared at her, pressing a finger firmly to his lips. Then he hopped onto an exposed wooden beam that led out into the darkness, striding along it like a rope-walker. Elio tested the beam, making sure it would support his weight. Then he started forwards, staying on his knees, inching into the dark.

He'd never been fond of heights, and it didn't help that he couldn't even see the ground. He squinted down into the shadows, trying to make out any kind of recognisable shape. The mysterious rumbling sound continued, and as his eyes adjusted he saw movement. Was that a tail, twitching? And there a head, the light reflected from an exposed fang?

Then realisation came, and he had to grab the beam to stop himself from falling. Those were Skaven down there, hundreds of them, all piled on top of each other. They were fast asleep, their snores filling the darkened space. This was a barracks-nest.

Elio urged himself to take a breath, to stay calm. The ragged boy beckoned frantically and he forced himself onwards. The beam branched and the boy took the right-hand way.

Elio braced and looked back, seeing
the others behind him in the gloom.
Their faces were pale – they'd seen
the Skaven. He was embarrassed to
discover that he was the only one on
his knees.

A shaft of crystal light made a circle
on the floor and in it he could see a
tangle of Skaven bodies, many still
clutching their swords. One reached
up to scratch its nose and Elio froze.
If it happened to wake at this exact
moment...

Then he heard a quiet cough and looked up. The boy crouched a short distance ahead beside a small hatch in the wall. Elio gritted his teeth and shuffled forwards, reaching the hatch and pulling himself through with trembling hands.

He dropped beside the boy, looking around. They were in a low-ceilinged corridor beside a pair of doors leading back into the barracks-nest. Ahead of them was the sprawling, ramshackle palace itself.

The interior was just as tatty as the outside – the roof was full of holes and the walls were off-kilter, leaning together at the top. Elio stepped backwards and almost cried out; there was a huge hole in the floor, its edges slick with rot.

'This place could use a lick of paint,' Kiri said, climbing down beside him.

'It's messier than my room at the Arbour,' Kaspar agreed.

The ragged boy took hold of Elio's

sleeve, tugging him forwards. They
turned into another hallway with
doors on either side, and peering
through them Elio saw a series of
large, misshapen rooms, their walls
off balance, their roofs patched or
missing. One seemed to be a dining
hall, the long table piled with scraps
of discarded meat. Flies buzzed around,
and the stench made him nauseous.
Beyond that was some kind of gallery,
the walls festooned with garish
paintings plundered from other, more

artistically inclined races.

The next corridor ran along the outer edge of the building, overlooking the cavern. But parts of the wall had fallen away, and beneath them Elio could see the ring of green braziers and the cliff below. He moved cautiously, testing every step. One rotten plank and he'd plummet to his death.

The boy had darted ahead, rounding a last corner and vanishing from view. Elio picked up the pace, turning to find himself facing a grand, misshapen entranceway with wooden doors hung unevenly. Torches guttered on the wall and the ceiling was black with soot.

They crept closer. There was no sign of the boy, but from inside a voice could be heard. Elio peered around the door.

The chamber within was impressively large, the walls painted in random splashes of colour. A moth-eaten chair stood before an empty fireplace and a golden chandelier hung from the ceiling, making it bow inwards. On the far side of the room Elio could see Kreech, his back to them, facing towards a curtained alcove in the wall. His hands were clasped and he was speaking in a low voice.

'My prize,' he beamed, gazing into the alcove. 'So precious, so fine-fine. And all mine, yes-yes. All mine.' He puffed on a warpstone pipe, and once again Elio noticed that the crystal was purple rather than green. 'They all thought I was mad-mad, didn't they?' Kreech went on. 'They said it was foolishness, getting involved with man-things. But I showed them, yes-yes.'

Elio took a bold step forward. His master was in that alcove, he was sure of it. Vertigan must be gagged or unconscious, unable to answer back. But he was there.

Kreech rubbed his paws together and Elio took another step, making fists of his trembling hands.

'Skaven,' he said and the packlord

whipped round, eyes glittering. 'We've come for our master, you foul creature. We demand that you give him back.'

CHAPTER SIX

Warpstone

A dreadful smile broke across Kreech's face, exposing his slavering fangs.
He started to shudder, letting out a squeaking, wheezing noise. It took Elio a moment to realise that the packlord was laughing.

'Oh, yes-yes!' Kreech cackled, clapping his hands. 'Oh good-good! One, two, three little precious presents, all wrapped up and delivered right to my great-grand chamber!'

'We're not joking,' Elio said, the others advancing either side of him. 'We've come to take Vertigan home.'

Kreech laughed again, a tear rolling

down his furred cheek. 'Of course you have, man-thing. You're so brave, aren't you? So fierce-fierce! I almost wish I hadn't sold your master so he could see-see your faces.'

Elio's mouth dropped. 'S-sold him? What do you mean?'

'I mean what I say!' Kreech snorted. 'I sold him, and look what he bought! So fine-fine! So beautiful!'

He stepped aside and there in the alcove was a huge warpstone crystal, pulsating with a sickly purple light. It was taller than Kreech himself, jagged and rough-hewn, its glow filling the room.

'Isn't it good-good?' the Skaven asked. 'Isn't it majestic? And just think, if this is my price for one old man-thing, imagine what she'll pay me for you!'

'*She?*' Kiri demanded, stepping forwards. 'Who is *she*?'

Kreech wagged a claw. 'That's not for you to know. Kreech can keep a secret, yes-yes.' He tugged on a rope and a tattered velvet curtain slid across the alcove, hiding the warpstone. The packlord took another pull on his pipe, the gleam reflected in his empty black eyes.

'Where is Vertigan now?' Elio asked. 'Tell us!'

'No-no, enough talk,' Kreech smirked. 'You'll find out soon-soon. Ah, look. It's my faithful pet.'

A figure bounded forwards, grabbing the Skaven's cloak and rubbing his face lovingly against it. It was the ragged boy, gurgling happily as Kreech patted him on the head. The boy pointed to the children, then to himself, grinning proudly.

'Yes-yes, clever Scratch,' Kreech said. 'You found them and brought them quick-quick to your master. Here is a special prize of your own, yes-yes.' He drew a lump of ripe-smelling cheese from a pouch at his waist, tossing it on the floor. The boy fell on it ferociously, scoffing it down and letting out a loud, rattling burp.

'He's yours?' Kiri asked in amazement. 'Your pet? But why–'

'Because of this,' Kreech said, grabbing the boy and turning his wrist, exposing the black mark. 'You knew he bore the sign, yes-yes? A special child.'

'A special child who betrayed us,' Elio muttered.

'He is my little secret,' Kreech went on, patting the boy's head. 'Kept safe-safe. Kept hidden, until the time comes. My prisoner, just like you.'

Elio felt a rush of anger. 'We're nobody's prisoner,' he snarled. 'Especially not a foul thing like you.'

And he started forward, Vertigan's staff raised. Scratch sprang clear as Elio lunged at Kreech, striking down with all his might. Kiri aimed her catapult and Kaspar darted low, grabbing for the packlord's tail.

But Kreech was too quick, and far too strong – he wrenched the staff from Elio's hand, using it to shove Kaspar back and block Kiri's catapult shot in a single, effortless movement. His tail lashed like a whip, wrapping around Elio's throat and forcing him to the ground. Kreech dropped the staff and stood over him, his humour utterly gone. The tail tightened and Elio coughed, clawing feebly.

'You may be brave, man-thing,' the Skaven hissed. 'But you are so very-very stupid.' The tail tightened, lifting Elio off his feet. 'The Skaven are the quick-smartest creatures in all the realms, and I, Kreech, am the quick-smartest of all the Skaven. Nobody challenges me. Nobody outwits me. Nobody!'

He took a breath, steadying himself. 'I am a sophisticated creature,' he muttered, as though talking to himself. 'I am cultured. I am wise. I have a gallery. I don't kill man-things while there is still a chance to profit from them. Five little prizes will fetch a pretty price.'

The tail unravelled and Elio fell

to the floor, his breath coming in hoarse gulps. Kiri dropped to his side, glowering at Kreech.

'We won't go quietly. Whoever this *she* is, we'll—'

'Wait,' Kaspar said, fear on his face. 'Did... did he say five?'

'Oh, yes.' Kreech smirked gleefully, reaching for a rope overhead. 'I almost forgot.'

A bell rang in the hallway and moments later they heard marching feet. In strode the portly Skaven, backed by a battalion of heavily armoured warriors. Several were larger than the regular ratmen, with pale fur and keen black claws. Stormvermin, Elio knew. The Skaven heavy infantry.

There were two other figures with them, with sacks over their heads and ropes binding their hands. Lesh reached up to tug the hoods free, but Elio had already recognised Thanis's breastplate and Alish's tool belt. They stood blinking, their faces red.

'What happened?' Kiri asked. 'We thought you were off in the tunnels.'

'We followed that little traitor,' Alish said, jerking her chin towards the ragged boy who sat grinning by the fireplace. 'He called the patrol on us. What about you?'

Kiri sighed. 'We trusted him too.'

Elio felt a sickening sense of failure as he realised they were trapped, wholly in Kreech's power. Every choice he'd made had been a mistake, every turn a wrong one. Bred to rule? Born to take charge? His father would laugh if he could see him now.

Then a thought struck him and he struggled to his feet, turning towards Kreech.

'I could pay you, you know,' he said. 'Maybe not in warpstone but in gold and jewels. Enough that you could buy this crystal ten times over.' He had no idea what the going rate was for giant warpstone shards, but the Skaven would pay more attention if he sounded like he knew what he was talking about.

'You make big promises, man-thing,' Kreech sneered, leaning closer. 'But your master is gone-gone, and I saw the palace where you dwell. It is a ruin.'

Elio swallowed. He hadn't wanted the others to find out this way, but he didn't have a choice. 'My father is the Lord of Lifestone,' he said, drawing the medallion from beneath his robes and holding it up. 'I'm Lord Elias's heir. He'll pay to get me back. My friends as well.'

He heard Alish gasp; Thanis's eyes widened, and even Kiri seemed shocked. But Kreech just folded his claws together, studying Elio keenly.

'So if I take you to your father he'll pay for your life, yes-yes? He'll give gold to a Skaven?'

Elio nodded. 'He'd do anything to keep me safe.'

Kreech pondered. 'Well, man-thing, this is interesting, yes-yes. A bargain with the Lord of Lifestone himself. Riches for Kreech, and freedom for his little lordling, yes-yes.' Then he frowned. 'But how do I know he would pay-pay? How do I know he wouldn't call his man-thing warriors and tell them to stamp out poor Kreech and his Skaven?'

'We could work out a plan,' Elio said hurriedly. 'Trust me, we could—'

Kreech shook his head. 'I already know who to trust-trust. She gave me one prize, she will give more. Better one warpstone crystal clutched in the claw than five still buried in the rock, as they say.' He gestured to Lesh. 'Take them to the dungeon. Quick-quick!'

The fat Skaven lumbered forwards, claws raised, but before he could reach them Kiri had whipped out her catapult, loading it and taking aim. Thanis followed her lead, slamming back into a large Skaven, lowering her head to butt another. Alish struggled with her bonds and Elio snatched up Vertigan's staff, gripping it defensively. He looked around, sure for a moment that something was wrong, something was missing.

'Fools-fools,' the packlord said as his warriors moved in. 'You think four man-thing children can stand against the power of Clan Quickfang and the mighty Kr–' He stopped abruptly, counting on his claws. 'Two, yes-yes, and three.' Then his head snapped up. 'There were five. I counted five. The quiet boy. Where is he?'

Elio whipped round. Kreech was right, Kaspar was gone. Somehow he had slipped away, without any of them noticing. Elio felt his face go red.

'He left us. The stinking coward!'

'No,' Thanis said in disbelief. 'He wouldn't, I know him.'

'Find that boy!' Kreech cried, waving a furious paw. 'He can't have gone far, just find hi–'

There was a swish of cloth and soft purple light flooded the room. Kreech turned in horror as his warpstone was revealed. Beside it stood Kaspar, one arm leaning on the huge crystal.

'Looking for me?' he grinned.

The Skaven soldiers gaped in wonder, Lesh's mouth dropping open with an audible thunk. Elio realised what was happening – Kreech hadn't told them about the enormous crystal, they were seeing it for the first time and their tiny rat minds could barely comprehend it.

The packlord gave a wail, striding towards the alcove. But Kaspar held up a firm hand.

'Stay where you are, or lose your prize.' He bounced on his heels and the floorboards groaned, the crystal rocking back and forth. It looked as though a few good kicks would take the floor out completely, sending the crystal plummeting to the cliffs below.

Kreech skidded to a halt, trembling with anger and shock. His soldiers crowded closer, drooling. Elio could see a purple gleam reflected in every eye, and one whispered, 'Sweet-sweet.'

'Back-back!' Kreech ordered. 'All of

you. Do as I say or there will be punishment!'

But the Skaven didn't move, they were utterly mesmerised.

'Let my friends go,' Kaspar said. 'Or I'll drop it.'

'No-no, don't be hasty,' Kreech said. 'Keep calm-calm and we can reach an agreement.'

'Let them go!' Kaspar demanded, slamming his heel into the floor. One of the planks snapped, tumbling into the darkness. The crystal lurched sideways, ready to fall.

Kreech gave a hiss of horror. Then he held up both hands, smiling from ear to ear. 'Of course, they can go. Of course, of course.' He waved to Lesh. 'Back-back. Let them through.'

The Skaven warriors parted sleepily, opening a passage to the door. Elio took hold of Alish and they stepped into the corridor of fur, Thanis and Kiri following. The ratmen were so transfixed they barely seemed to notice.

Scratch crouched in the doorway, glaring at them in confusion.

'We should take him back with us,' Alish said. 'Like we planned.'

Thanis nodded, taking the boy firmly by the arm. 'We're taking your pet,' she told Kreech. 'He's one of us, remember?'

The packlord tore his eyes from the crystal. 'But he's mine. This wasn't part of the bargain.'

'It is now,' Kaspar said, and gave the floor another kick. There was a groan and Elio heard three loud snaps. The crystal leaned further, and Kreech gave a shriek.

'Take-take!' he said. 'The man-thing is yours. He's no use anyway, not without your master.'

'We'll find him too,' Alish said. 'You'll see.'

They backed into the corridor. Through the cluster of silhouetted Skaven Elio could still see Kaspar, poised in the alcove. 'Wait,' he called. 'What about you? How are you meant to get out?'

But Kaspar just grinned. 'This way,' he said, and gave one last kick.

The boards broke. The crystal dropped from sight. And Kaspar fell too, dropping feet first into the dark. Through a gap in the floor Elio saw him for a moment, outlined in the crystal flare. Then the shadows claimed him and he disappeared.

Alish gave a cry, but it was drowned by a shriek of absolute horror as Kreech saw his crystal hit the rocks, exploding into a thousand shards like a violet firecracker. The fragments tumbled down the cliff face, spinning and sparkling as they fell. The packlord ran to the alcove, his mouth open in shock and despair. He looked down into the hole, unable to believe what was happening.

Then the other Skaven began to swarm towards the alcove, snapping hungrily. Kreech waved his arms, trying to hold them back. 'No-no!' he shouted. 'Seize the man-things! Do as I say!'

But his soldiers shoved past him, leaping down through the hole like sailors fleeing a burning ship. Elio saw them land on the rocks, a furry tide bounding and chasing after the shards of falling warpstone. A few were so eager they missed the peak altogether, crashing straight down the cliff with a wail of surprise. But the rest clung on, springing from rock to rock and from precipice to precipice, hunting the gleaming fragments.

Kreech looked back, and his eyes were wild. A few warriors remained – Lesh and a handful of others, too scared to take the wild plunge down the cliff side.

'Fools-fools,' he cried, pointing at Elio and his friends. 'Don't just stand there gawping. Grab them!'

CHAPTER SEVEN

Stray Sparks

Elio raced along the hallway. He could
hear the Skaven coming in pursuit,
their claws clattering on the rickety
boards. Through gaps in the wall he
could see down to the black cliff, lit
with sparks of purple like jewels in the
darkness. He looked for Kaspar but the
shadows were too deep.

Alish's face was wet with tears.
'Kaspar, he...' she spluttered. 'He just...'

'He'll be all right,' Thanis said,
dragging the writhing, kicking Scratch.
'He's clever and he's tough.' But Elio
could hear the doubt in her voice.

Kiri halted suddenly, listening. The

floor shook; more footsteps were approaching from the other direction, from the barracks-nest. Her eyes darted left and right. There: an open doorway.

She darted through, the others following. It was the room with the dining table, the length of it scattered with chunks of rotten, half-chewed meat. The stench was incredible, the air thick with flies. Elio held his breath, ducking beneath the table. Thanis cursed as Scratch lashed at her, wrapping her hand over his mouth to stifle his cries. All was suddenly silent.

The two Skaven search parties met in the corridor.

'Where have they gone?' Kreech demanded. 'The little sneak-thieves. I want them back-back!'

'Lord Kreech, why are these man-things so important?' Lesh asked. 'S-surely we should be trying to recover your beautiful warpstone?'

'Fool-fool!' Kreech said. 'With those children we can get more warpstone.

Much more!'

'But-but...' Lesh stammered, confused. 'There is warpstone right there, I see it. The warpstone you speak of is not there. It is... somewhere else. Why should we not just take this warpstone?'

There was a thud and a loud *oof* of pain. 'Don't try to think-think,' Kreech hissed. 'It does not suit you.' He was silent for a moment, tapping one claw thoughtfully. 'I have it,' he said at last. 'Come-come, all of you. They took a different route from my chambers. They must be trying to escape.'

'But-but, surely they'll try to reach the rail-carts?' Lesh said. 'That would seem the most—'

There was another thud, and the fat Skaven gave a deep, agonised groan.

'I warned you,' Kreech sneered. 'Now quick-quick, that way!'

They moved off and Kiri looked at Elio. 'Right, what now?'

Elio hung his head, unable to meet

her eye. 'I don't want to be in charge any more. I've made such a mess of things – every decision I've made has been a disaster. And now Kaspar... now he's...'

'Don't say it,' Kiri said. 'Kaspar's sneaky, he'll have had a plan. And you can't blame yourself. Coming here was the right thing to do. We had to try to rescue Vertigan, and look how far we came. Plus we found the seventh mark. If we can get Scratch back to the Arbour this won't have been a waste. I think Vertigan would be proud of us. All of us.'

Elio bit his lip. 'You think so?'

'I'm sure of it,' Kiri said. 'Now, Alish, take a look outside and see if they're really gone. All the Skaven in the barracks will either be chasing after us or hunting down that warpstone, and Kreech went the other way – we heard him. If we can make it back to the carts we might still have a chance.'

Alish slipped out from under the

table, tiptoeing to the door. 'It's clear,' she whispered.

They crept along the hall, turning into the corridor that led to the barracks-nest. They could hear the chatter of Skaven out on the cliffside, but here in the hallway it was quiet.

One of the barracks doors stood wide, and beyond it was blackness. Kiri beckoned, and one by one they crept inside. The smell was overwhelming, but there was no sound of snoring. 'Stay close and go as quick as you can,' she whispered.

The room wasn't totally dark, the crystal light slanting pale through the ceiling cracks. Elio felt something around his feet and realised they were wading through piles of moulted Skaven fur, a rough carpet covering the floor. He shivered in disgust.

But Kiri's hunch seemed right – the barracks were deserted. They weaved between wooden pillars, moving in complete silence. Then she slowed.

'There's the window we climbed through. Which means the door to the storeroom should be just... here.' Elio heard rattling, and Kiri cursed.

'What's going on?' he asked.

'It's barred from the outside,' she said. Why would they...'

'To keep you from getting out, yes-yes,' a voice said, and they whipped round.

A purple gleam lit the shadows, wreathed in smoke. Kreech took a puff on his warpstone pipe, illuminating the ten or more soldiers gathered around him.

'Once again, you thought you were so quick-smart,' he said. 'And again, you were so-so wrong. Of course you would come this way – how else would you escape? But now you're caught-caught, with nowhere to run.'

He gestured to a pair of bright-eyed Skaven and they each took a step forwards, flanking their packlord. One raised a long-barrelled musket, the other crouching down to hold the barrel steady. Elio had read about Skaven rifles in Vertigan's book – warplock jezzails, he'd called them, and they fired bullets made of polished warpstone.

Thanis tightened her grip, clinging to Scratch as he squirmed and thrashed. 'We still have your boy. Shoot at us and you might hit him too.'

Kreech snorted. 'Oh, girl-thing, he's just a pet. You think I care if he lives or dies?'

Scratch stared at his master, hurt shining in his eyes.

'You're a beast,' Thanis said.

'No-no,' Kreech snapped, bitterness in his voice. 'You are the beasts. You destroyed my beautiful prize, after I worked so hard-hard to get it. Any other Skaven would simply kill you for what you've done. But I am Kreech, the wise and benevolent. I shall restrain myself to merely selling you.'

'You'll have to catch us first,' Alish said, and her hand whipped out.

There was an eye-scorching flash and the Skaven warriors reeled back, screeching. Kreech recoiled, and Elio saw the sniper looking down at his musket in surprise.

Kiri aimed her catapult, taking a shot, and another. Two strangled cries rang out; one of them sounded like Lesh. Alish threw another flare, the Skaven shrinking back in shock.

'Thanis, give me the boy,' Kiri said, reaching for Scratch. 'Now see if that door's as badly made as everything else here.'

Thanis lowered her shoulders and

charged at the door, slamming into it with all her might. The wood shook and groaned, but it didn't break. Thanis drew back and charged again.

Kreech had recovered himself, turning on his soldiers as another of Alish's bolts sent shadows dancing up the walls. 'It's just a flash-flash, it can't hurt you! Stop cowering and seize them, before I– Eeeeegh!'

He sprang suddenly into the air, shrieking and whirling around. His soldiers drew back in confusion as Kreech spun again, his hands flapping madly. On the third turn Elio saw what had caused the packlord to panic. Kreech's tail was on fire, flames coursing through his dry fur. The floor beneath his feet was alive with sparks, black smoke coiling up into the room.

'Throw another bolt,' Elio urged Alish. 'Over there, behind them.'

Alish grinned, rifling in her pouch and tossing bolt after bolt. The fur-strewn floor soon ignited, flames leaping

towards the ceiling. The Skaven soldiers
huddled together, frightened by the
flames. Kreech squealed in pain and
anger, batting at his smouldering tail.

Then there was a crash and the doors
flew open, Thanis slamming through
into the storeroom beyond. 'Come on!'
she shouted.

But the flames had spread too quickly;
between them and the door was a wall
of fire. Kiri put her head down and leapt
through, clutching Scratch as the flames
licked at her clothes. The boy screamed,

bucking wildly, and Elio thought he
was trying to return to his master.
Then he saw Kiri patting Scratch's arm,
extinguishing the flames that had licked
at his dry clothes. His skin was scorched,
his face twisted in pain.

Elio drew back but Alish grabbed his
arm. 'It's just one jump. You can do
this, come on.'

She gritted her teeth and bounded
through the flames, but Elio just
clutched the staff, willing himself to
follow her. The Skaven were shrieking
behind him as the barracks blazed.
His pulse was racing, but somewhere
down deep he felt a little of his old
confidence returning. They'd come this
far, and now they were almost free. If
he got a little singed, so be it.

With a whoop he slammed the staff
into the floorboards, using it to vault
himself up and over the raging fire. He
felt the flames singe his cloak as he
soared through the air, then he hit the
ground and ran.

CHAPTER EIGHT
Runaway

Elio piled into the empty rail-cart,
joining the others as they crouched
inside, trying to use their body weight
to get the cart moving. But it just
rocked on its wheels, refusing to budge.

'Everybody hang on,' Thanis said,
jumping out onto the tracks. 'I've got
this.'

She unhooked the chain connecting
them to the second cart then she put
her shoulder against the backboard and
pushed, her boots struggling for grip
on the smooth steel rails. The axles
groaned and the wheels creaked, but
they began to roll slowly forwards.

Then there was a deafening noise and something thudded into the side of the cart, splintering the wood. In the barracks doorway Elio could see the Skaven marksmen, their musket barrel smoking. Kreech pushed past them, coughing and hacking. Flames rose behind him and Lesh hurried forwards, patting his master's smouldering pelt.

But the cart was gaining momentum now, rolling towards the opening in the storeroom wall. Elio ducked as they emerged into the cavern, the tracks following the side of the storeroom then disappearing over the edge of the cliff. Thanis kept pushing, her muscles straining, her face red with exertion. Behind her Elio could see Kreech leaping into the second cart, Lesh and the marksmen tumbling in after him. The packlord waved his arms, and two of his warriors began to push.

'They're coming after us,' Elio told Thanis. 'Quick!'

She scowled up at him. 'I'm doing...

my best,' she managed between shoves.
'Feel free... to help.'

'No need,' Alish said, her eyes wide.
'Time to jump in!'

The cart began to tip, the wheels
rolling slowly, sickeningly over the edge.
Thanis hoisted herself up, tumbling in
beside Scratch as he cowered in the
base of the cart, clutching his scorched
arm. The carriage tilted forwards, the
rails groaned beneath them, and they
were away.

As a boy Elio had loved to ride his

father's horse, spurring the stallion as fast as he could and feeling the thrill in his belly as they broke into a gallop. This was similar, but a hundred times more terrifying. The cart picked up speed, wheels clattering on the rails. Elio clung to the front, his knuckles turning white. Beside him Alish let out a holler of excitement, her hair streaming out behind her. 'Isn't this great?' she yelled, and Elio tried not to whimper.

All the way down the cliff he could see bands of Skaven still scrambling after the loose warpstone, the black rock scattered with shards like purple stars in a night-time sky. Others were clambering up from the base of the cavern, bounding hungrily over the rocks.

Then a musket roared and Elio ducked as the bullet whined overhead. The second cart came thundering after them, Kreech upright in the prow. Beyond him Elio could see the blazing barracks, flames leaping towards the ceiling. Black smoke rose into the cavern.

The snipers crouched beside their packlord, the musket steadied on the front of the cart. One took aim, his finger tightening on the trigger.

'Down!' Elio shouted, but the musket was already firing, smoke billowing from the stock. The bullet was on target but the cart tipped clear just in time, two wheels leaving the track as they took the first bend at full speed. The shot missed them by a whisker, cracking into the rock.

'Everyone, to the side!' Alish yelled, throwing herself over. Thanis and Kiri leaned hard, counterbalancing the cart as it screeched round the corner, sparks flying. Scratch was thrown from one side to the other, landing on his scorched arm and letting out a cry of pain. Then the wheels righted and they were back on the slope, picking up speed.

Elio crouched, reaching under his cloak and unclipping his satchel. He rifled inside, pulling out a small pot of black unguent. He reached for Scratch's arm but the boy pulled away, whining. Elio fixed him with a calming stare.

'I'm not going to hurt you,' he said. 'I'm going to help you.'

He dipped his fingers in the ointment, holding them out for Scratch to smell. Then he took hold of the boy's shoulder as the cart jounced and juddered, smearing the slippery substance as carefully as he could onto the boy's singed arm. Scratch winced, growling. Then his eyes widened in surprise as he saw the red colour fading.

Elio realised this might be the first time the boy had ever met a healer – he didn't know where he'd been before Kreech found him, but he doubted the packlord would care if Scratch got hurt. He felt a wave of sadness, and smiled as kindly as he could. Scratch beamed back, a dazzling grin despite his cracked teeth.

'Not bad for a lord's son,' Thanis said softly, and Elio looked up.

'I'm sorry I never told you,' he sighed. 'I just didn't want you to think I was different.'

Thanis laughed. 'We're all different. Maybe that's why we work so well together.'

Then Alish shouted, 'Hey! Out of the way!' and Elio sat up quickly.

On the track ahead a pair of familiar-looking Skaven were wrestling for a chunk of warpstone; one had a stump-tail, the other a grey stripe. Krat and Scowlish snarled at one another, neither willing to relinquish the precious purple fragment.

Then the sound of screeching wheels reached them and they looked up in horror, fumbling with the crystal, dropping it on the tracks. They were thrown back as the cart slammed through, the warpstone exploding in a cloud of fine purple dust. Krat and

Scowlish looked down in disbelief and disappointment, then went back to hitting each other.

Alish made sure they were ready for the second corner, ordering them into position as the cart screamed through the bend. Another musket shot barely missed them, Thanis cursing as she threw herself down. Kreech's cart was still coming after them, the packlord waving his arms.

'It's a clever system,' Alish said, her hair streaming out behind her. 'But it's really quite straightforward. I bet I could make one back in Lifestone.'

Elio snorted. 'If I never go near another rail-cart as long as I live, I'll be... What's wrong?'

Alish was staring down the track ahead of them, a look of pure horror on her face. Far below, Elio could see the third and final switchback, where the tracks turned towards the base of the cavern. But before they reached it they'd pass a junction, and it was this that had caught Alish's attention.

'That lever,' she said, pointing to a wooden bar jutting up beside the tracks. 'My guess is that it operates the turning. If that Skaven pulls it, we're in a lot of trouble.'

One of the ratmen was crouched beside the junction, both hands on the lever, struggling with it. Elio could see the branch line leading out into the cavern, along a stretch of rickety scaffold. Then with a gulp he noticed that the line was unfinished – it came to a dead stop, high above the floor of the cave. If they made that turning, they'd plummet to their deaths.

'What do we do?' he asked, trying to keep the panic from his voice. They were drawing closer, and still closer, the Skaven tugging furiously on the lever, straining with all its might.

'We hold on!' Alish said. 'And hope he doesn't– Oh.'

The mechanism gave out and the lever slammed down, the Skaven cackling victoriously. Elio clung on as the cart sped towards the turning.

CHAPTER NINE

Stampede

The Skaven turned to grin at them,
black eyes flashing. Another of the
ratmen came leaping down behind
it, hunched and swift in a long, grey
cloak. Coming to offer congratulations,
no doubt, Elio thought as the second
Skaven approached the first.

Then to his amazement it reached
out, grabbing the other by the tail and
yanking it backwards. The first Skaven
fell and the second bounded clear over
it, landing beside the lever. The cloaked
figure took hold, shoving with all its
might. Elio saw hands gripping the
wood. Hands with no claws.

The lever slammed back into place just as the cart came screaming through. Thanis reached out and the hooded figure grabbed her wrist, dragged clear off the ground as they flew by. Elio helped to haul him in, hearing the first Skaven scream in petulant fury.

Kaspar threw back his hood, grinning up at them. His hands were scratched and his lip was split but otherwise he looked unhurt.

'My plan worked, then. You all got away.'

Alish screamed in delight and Thanis pulled him in for a hug. 'How did you...? What did you...?'

'I grabbed one of the support posts as I fell,' Kaspar explained. 'The Skaven were so crazy for that warpstone they just dropped past me. I climbed down here, and as long as I kept my head covered they didn't even notice me. I've been hiding behind that rock waiting for you to come past.'

'What if we hadn't?' Kiri asked. 'What would you have done?'

Kaspar shrugged. 'I didn't even think about that. I knew you'd make it.'

They were so busy celebrating that the final corner took them completely by surprise, the cart almost overturning as it hit the bend. But Kiri and Thanis reacted quickly, leaning into the turn. Scratch almost tumbled out but Elio reached for his ankles just in time, hauling him back inside.

Then they were at the base of the cliff, and hurtling back onto the flat. Skaven stared up slack-jawed as they rattled past, black eyes widening even further when they saw Kreech and his warriors in pursuit. The packlord gestured furiously and some of them got the message, keeping pace with the speeding carriages.

Elio watched nervously. As long as the cart was still moving they were safe, but when they reached the end of the line they'd be in trouble. And now the marksmen were reloading their musket, trying to hold the powder horn steady as the cart shuddered. Far above them the mansion was blazing, the crystal's light cutting shafts through the churning smoke.

Then the gun roared, followed by a loud clang. Alish jerked round. 'They shot my hammer! How dare they?'

'Sooner or later they're going to hit one of us,' Kiri said. 'We need to do something.'

They were approaching the delivery platform, where the Skaven had tied on the second cart.

Thanis's eyes lit up. 'Elio, give me the staff. And Kiri, hold on to me.'

She took hold of Vertigan's staff, lifting it over her head and leaning as far as she could over the side of the cart. Kiri held tight to her legs as Thanis strained further, swinging the sturdy staff over her head, then down and around just as they reached the loading dock. The staff made contact and the platform exploded into fragments, boards splintering and spiralling up into the air, chunks of wood raining down onto the tracks behind them.

Kreech wailed in horror but there was nothing he could do. His cart slammed into the heap of planks and spun into the air, flipping end over end. Kreech was flung clear but some of the others weren't so lucky – Elio saw them hit the rails and then the cart crashed on top of them, wheels-up. A cloud of splinters and dust rose into the air, followed by Kreech's furious cries. Kiri hauled Thanis back inside as Kaspar grinned and Alish gave a cheer. The cart sped onwards through the cave.

Eventually they began to slow, gliding up a shallow rise then down towards the delver paddocks. Elio could see the creatures crowded in their pens, a sea of dark, hairy backs. Beyond them the ground sloped up towards the mouth of the tunnel, the one that would lead them home.

But their troubles were far from over. From behind came a din of shrieking and stamping, and glancing back he could see the Skaven swarming through the cavern, a seething tide of fur and teeth. It was going to be close.

The end of the line arrived without warning, the cart crashing through a wooden barrier and tipping nose first, throwing them clear. Elio tumbled head over feet, letting out a squawk

of surprise as he splashed into a large puddle of something warm, wet and stinking.

He sat up. Kiri lay beside him in the pool of delver manure. Thanis hung on to Scratch as he struggled to his feet then slipped back down again. Only Alish had avoided the puddle, sailing clean over to land on dry ground on the far side. She laughed as she hauled Kaspar out. 'You're all going straight in the bath when we get home,' she grinned, and Elio wondered if that was something her mother used to say. If Alish ever knew her mother; he'd never thought to ask.

He dug around in the muck, locating Vertigan's staff and wiping it on his robe. The stench was terrible, but at least they'd had a soft landing. Alish and Kaspar were already making for the tunnel, followed closely by Thanis and the boy. Elio looked back. The Skaven streamed in, massing for the attack. He started to run, Kiri on his heels.

Then he saw Alish freeze, taking a step back. Shapes loomed from the tunnel, striding towards them. A pack of stormvermin – at least ten, maybe more. They raced down the slope, their fangs bared, their armour glinting. Elio looked around desperately, scanning for another way out. But all he could see were the paddocks and the shack, the sheer black walls and the eyes of a thousand advancing Skaven. Many clutched fragments of warpstone, purple sparks glittering in the gloom.

Elio felt his hands shake, unable to fight down his fear. To have come so far, to be so close, it wasn't fair. There had to be a way. There had to be.

In the paddock the delvers muttered and raised their muzzled heads, sensing the approaching warpstone. And like light breaking through smoke, he knew what they had to do.

He grabbed Kiri, pulling her close. 'The delvers,' he said. 'They love warpstone. They'll do anything for it.'

The creatures snorted, pawing the ground. Kiri's eyes widened as she realised what he was getting at.

'Tell the others,' Elio said. 'This'll work.'

'What about you?' Kiri asked.

He looked down at the mob of ratmen, Kreech striding furiously at their head. 'I got us into this mess,' he said. 'So it's up to me to get us out again. I'll buy you as much time as I can.'

Kiri opened her mouth to protest, then she saw the determination in his eyes. 'Be careful.'

Elio smiled. 'Be quick-quick,' he said, and turned away.

He strode down the slope clutching the staff, his heart hammering like one of Alish's steam contraptions. He passed the shack, entering the courtyard in front. The Skaven advanced in a long, uneven line, grasping daggers and short-swords and gleaming muskets. Seeing Elio, Kreech held up a hand and

they halted, watching and chittering.
Beyond them in the heart of the cave
Elio could see the mansion still ablaze,
parts of the structure tumbling loose
and rolling down the cliff in a shower
of sparks.

'What do you want, young lordling?'
Kreech demanded. 'Come to beg-beg for
your pitiful lives?'

Elio shook his head. He had to drag
this out for as long as he could, to give
Kiri and the others time to execute his
plan. He could see them in the corner
of his eye, dark shapes creeping over
the fence into the delver paddock.

'I've come to bargain,' he said, fighting
to keep his voice steady, recalling his
lessons in elocution and leadership. 'Let
me and my friends go, and none of you
will be harmed.'

Kreech made a sound that was
somewhere between laughter, rage and
utter disbelief. 'Harmed?' he seethed,
barely able to get the word out.
Then his voice shot up in volume,

spittle flying from his jaws. '*Harmed?*
Man-thing, you are sick-sick in the
head if you think you can threaten me.
You come here, shatter my prize, burn
my beautiful home, make fool-fools out
of my soldiers and you have the nerve
to threaten me? I will make you all
beg for mercy, just as soon as I find
your man-thing friends.'

He raised his snout, black eyes
darting towards the paddock. Without
thinking, Elio lunged towards Kreech
and grabbed his arm, yanking the
Skaven back to face him.

'Hey,' he shouted. 'Don't worry about
them. I'm the one you want.'

The surrounding ratmen gave a gasp
of horror – no one laid hands on their
packlord.

Kreech jerked back, shaking Elio off.
'You dare to touch me? Do you want
me to kill-kill you, is that it? Do you
think that by taunting me you can
drive me to anger, that I will spare
your pain?' He took a long pull on

his pipe, trembling with fury. The warpstone gleamed, smoke trailing into the air. Then Kreech gestured, 'Take him, quick-quick.'

Two Skaven scurried forwards – Krat and Scowlish, their eyes blazing with bitterness over the lost warpstone. They took hold of Elio's arms, forcing him to drop the staff. But he didn't struggle, facing Kreech without blinking. *Wait*, he thought suddenly. *Am I being brave?* He was absolutely terrified, every nerve in his body jangling. But beneath it all there was a calm voice telling him what to do. Vertigan's voice? Partly. But his own voice, too.

Kreech reached into the bowl of his pipe, plucking out the fragment of warpstone with his long claws. 'Beautiful, yes-yes,' he said, his eyes glowing with reflected light. 'Warpstone can be used for many purposes, man-thing. For spell-magic. For pipe-smoke. And for inflicting pain.'

He leaned in, the fragment clutched

in his pincer-like grip. Elio tried to pull
away but the arms holding him were
too strong. Somewhere in the distance
he heard the drum of heavy, lumbering
feet.

Then it was like a fire had been lit
inside his skull as Kreech pressed the
warpstone into his forehead. Elio heard
himself cry out, heard the packlord
cackling with delight. Kreech returned
the warpstone crumb to his pipe, letting
the smoke wreathe around his head.

'I told you, man-thing.' He smiled

as Krat and Scowlish let go, dropping Elio in the mud. 'You should not play with– Aaagh!'

The Skaven flung his arms up in terror as a wall of black thundered through the courtyard. Huge feet pounded the earth and Elio felt the ground shaking, cries erupting all around him. *They did it*, he thought through the hammering in his skull. *They really did it. And now I'm going to get completely flattened.*

He rolled over, pressing his face into the mud as the Deepearth Delvers stampeded over him, charging at the terrified Skaven. He felt a clawed foot scrape his shoulder and another slam into his back, driving the air from his lungs. But the creatures were moving so fast that the pressure was only fleeting; moments later they had passed on, leaving him miraculously unharmed.

He sat up, blinking. The pain in his head was still there, but it was starting to fade. Around him all was

chaos. Kiri and the others had removed
the delvers' muzzles and opened the
paddock gates, unleashing the creatures
on the Skaven and their warpstone.
Now the beasts were ploughing into
the ranks of the ratmen, charging at
anyone in possession of the smallest
crumb of the purple crystal.

Elio saw one of the creatures using
its tentacled snout to pull warpstone
from the hand of an unconscious
Skaven, chomping it down with a
sound like shattering glass. A group of
armed ratmen were trying to drive the
delvers back with swords and pikes,
but two of the beasts ran at them from
behind, scattering them like skittles.
The floor of the courtyard was littered
with shards of warpstone and the
delvers moved back and forth, tentacles
twitching, sucking up the crumbs. One
of them lifted its snout and let out a
burbling cry that sounded a lot like joy.

Then Elio heard a shout and saw
Kreech advancing once more, a sword

in his hand. He was covered from
snout to tail in mud, his lips drawn
back in a sneer of pure animal rage.
'Man-thing!' he bellowed. 'Prepare to d–'

The delver came out of nowhere,
hurtling like a rock down a mountain.
Kiri clung to its back, raising her fist
and whooping like a dragon-rider. One
minute Kreech was there, sprinting at
Elio with murder in his eyes. Then
there was a thud and a wail, and he
was gone.

Kiri dropped from the delver's back,

hurrying closer. 'Come on,' she said.
'We're leaving.'

She grabbed Vertigan's staff, pressing
it into his hand. Elio staggered up, and
for a moment the world spun. 'Are you
all right?' Kiri asked, peering at the
burn on his forehead. 'Can you walk?'

Elio put a hand on her shoulder. 'I'm
okay, just shaky. It doesn't even hurt
that much.'

They jogged up the slope, joining the
others at the edge of the paddock.

'What you did was incredible,' Alish
said.

'Agreed,' Kaspar said. 'Risking your life
like that, it was really brave.'

Elio blushed. 'Well, you did it first.'

Thanis stood in the entrance to the
tunnel, holding Scratch by the wrist.
The boy stared back into the cave with
huge eyes, but he didn't try to resist.
They'd take him back to the Arbour,
and figure out what to do next.

There was a shout below them and
a group of six Skaven came racing up

the slope. Elio gripped the staff but the ratmen didn't even look at them, fleeing into the tunnel. They were all clutching fragments of warpstone; one was the size of Elio's head.

Then the floor shook as three delvers broke from the main pack – they'd spotted the fleeing Skaven and now they came lumbering up the slope, hoofs pounding. Elio and the others scrambled back as the delvers thundered past, shoving into the passage. The walls shook, chunks of earth raining down.

'Quick,' Kiri shouted. 'They're going to bring the whole tunnel down.'

They ran inside, the entrance crumbling behind them. Darkness fell but they kept moving, hearing the delvers up ahead, shaking the walls and the roof as they plunged on. Elio flinched as a clod of earth clipped his shoulder, shattering on the ground.

Then there was a cry of pain and he whirled round. He couldn't see anything

but he could hear Thanis cursing, and
the sounds of a struggle.

'Alish!' he shouted. 'The Bolts of Azyr!'

In the flash that followed Elio saw
Thanis clinging desperately to Scratch
as he tugged and fought. There was
blood on her arm and the boy's teeth
were bared. Then it was dark again.

'I lost him!' Thanis cried. 'Don't let
him get away!'

Alish threw another bolt, lighting up
Scratch as he sprinted towards another
opening in the earth. Thanis started
after him but then Elio heard an
ominous creak overhead.

'Wait!' he shouted. 'It's too dangerous!'

The roof of the tunnel crashed in,
the roar filling Elio's ears. He covered
his head, breathing earth and dust.
As the din faded Alish threw another
bolt. Thanis stood alone beside a heap
of fallen earth. There was no sign of
Scratch.

'We have to find him,' Thanis cried,
and Elio heard her scraping at the

dirt, digging into it with her hands. 'We have to get him back.'

'There's no time,' Kiri said. 'We have to go before they find us.'

'Why did he run?' Thanis asked bitterly. 'We could've helped him. We were so close to getting something good out of all this.'

'I think he was scared,' Alish said. 'Kreech has looked after him, and he only just met us. I can kind of understand it.'

Elio reached into his pocket for the Light of Teclis. 'Well, we can't wait for them to find us. Come on, let's hope this thing still works.'

CHAPTER TEN

The Siege

They struggled out through the hole in the Atheneum floor, groaning and coughing dust. Elio pocketed the Light of Teclis; the pain in his head had faded but he still felt strange and uneasy, like he was seeing everything from a distance. Thanis mopped her brow, still bitter over the loss of Scratch. Kaspar stood apart, blinking as though trying to process everything that had happened. Alish lay flat on the tiles, smiling up at the dome overhead.

'Home,' she said with relief.

Kiri stood beside Elio, taking his arm. 'We survived,' she said. 'Thanks to you.'

'But we didn't get Vertigan back. And we didn't bring Scratch with us either.'

'But we know where he is now,' Alish pointed out. 'The seventh mark. That's got to be important.'

'I'm not going back to get him,' Kaspar said. 'Just so you know.'

Thanis sighed, looking utterly defeated. Elio looked at the staff in his hand, then he held it out to her. 'You should have this. You're better with it than I am. I think Vertigan would've wanted it.'

'You're sure?' Thanis asked, a smile playing around her lips. 'I mean, if my lord commands it...'

Elio sighed. 'That's never going away, is it? Honestly, I'm a completely normal person, just like you.'

'Only with more servants,' Alish grinned.

'And fancier clothes,' Kiri added.

'And golden silverware,' Kaspar laughed.

'That doesn't even make any sense!'

Elio protested. 'How can you have golden s—'

A bolt of pain blazed behind his eyes, leaving him gasping. Kiri peered at him, frowning.

'I don't like that burn. It's... funny-looking.'

'What sort of funny-looking?' Elio asked, crossing his eyes and trying to look upwards.

Alish fetched a mirror from her workbench and Elio squinted into it. Kiri was right, the mark did look strange. The burn was bright red as you'd expect, but there were little purple traces snaking from it like vines beneath the skin.

'Vertigan's book said warpstone is unpredictable,' he said, poking at his forehead. 'The Skaven use it for all sorts of weird magics. And it can change people. Mutate them.'

Thanis peered at him. 'Do you feel like you're mutating?'

Elio frowned. 'Mostly it doesn't even

hurt, just these flashes. I do feel sort of far away, but I'm probably just tired.'

Kiri shook her head. 'I think we should take you to a healer.'

Alish sighed. 'In Lifestone? There are no healers left. No decent ones, anyway.'

'Wouldn't your father know someone?' Thanis asked. 'Someone from before, maybe?'

'I'm not asking my father for help,' Elio said quickly. 'I haven't even spoken to him in months. He hates me for joining Vertigan.'

'I'm sure he doesn't *hate* you,' Alish said. 'Maybe if we just–'

'No,' Elio insisted. 'Leave him out of this. Kaspar, what's wrong?'

The boy was standing with his head on one side, listening carefully. 'I thought I heard... but I'm not sure.'

Thanis looked at the hole in the floor. 'Is it Kreech? Is he coming for us?'

'That tunnel totally collapsed,' Kiri said. 'I don't see how he could follow us this quickly. Anyway, the last time

I saw him he was underneath one of those delvers.'

'I don't think it's the Skaven,' Kaspar said. 'It sounds like shouting. Lots of people shouting.'

Elio held his breath. All he could hear was the breeze rushing through the empty halls. Then he realised there were voices in it, so indistinct that they were almost part of the wind itself. There was a dull boom, like an explosion in the distance. They looked at one another.

'It's coming from the city,' Kaspar said. 'I'm sure of it.'

Alish nodded. 'Let's take a look.'

She unhooked a rope from the wall and high above them cogs began to creak. She tugged and a counterweight rose smoothly, a wooden platform descending towards them.

'Kiri, Elio, hop on,' Alish said. 'Just three at a time, it can't take any more.'

They climbed on and Alish let the rope out hand over hand.

'Where do you find time to make all this stuff?' Kiri asked.

Alish shrugged. 'I don't sleep much. And I wanted to be able to work on the top of my airship without letting all the air out.'

They reached the top, stepping onto a narrow balcony that ran around the inside of the dome. The glass was shaded in different colours, but they soon found a clear spot to peer through. Alish lowered the platform for the others, then she crouched beside Elio, gazing out.

Night had fallen, the city of Lifestone slumbering under a moonlit sky. Lanterns flickered in the nest of streets and torches glowed on the city walls. But they weren't the only source of light down there – far from it. In the dark beyond the wall a thousand fires blazed, ribbons of flame stretching out into the dark.

There was movement down there too, beyond the wall and atop it. Elio could

see tiny figures taking up positions
along the ramparts: the Lifestone
Defenders, manning the trebuchets and
stocking the quivers, ducking fearfully
behind the stone ramparts.

But their terror was entirely justified.
For outside the wall, filling the valley
from end to end and side to side, was
a vast, shadowed army. Elio couldn't
make out individual soldiers, just
shifting torches and black-clad shapes.
They were setting up attack engines
of their own; he saw giant catapults

standing out against the sky, and wooden stockades being raised on both sides of the river.

'What's...? Is that...? Who *is* that?' Alish managed as Kaspar and Thanis joined them, peering out.

'Whoever it is, they're not attacking,' Kiri said. 'Not yet, at least.'

Elio wondered where his father was – in the thick of it, most likely, risking his own life to save his men. He felt a flush of pride, remembering his own actions back in the warren. He wondered if he'd ever get the chance to tell Elias about it, and if his father would be proud.

'Could it be the Skaven?' Alish asked.

Elio shook his head. 'They wouldn't lay a siege like this. They'd just swarm in.'

Kiri sniffed the air. 'Do you smell that? It's... familiar somehow.'

Elio took a sniff. There was a strange scent on the air, faint but potent, like rot and damp earth.

Then he heard himself scream as another bolt of pain ripped through his skull without warning. He toppled over, the dome spinning above him, his limbs twitching uncontrollably. Kiri grabbed him, laying him down on his back. This time it didn't abate but grew more intense, tearing through his head like hot irons, scattering his thoughts until all he knew was pain.

'What's happening?' Alish cried.

'I don't know,' Kiri said. 'But it's getting worse.'

'His burn,' Thanis said, pointing. 'It's glowing.'

Elio looked up desperately, blinking through the agony in his head. Kiri and Thanis bent over him, their faces filled with fear and concern. Alish and Kaspar knelt beside them, each taking one of his hands. Their presence calmed him, helped him force back his fear. They had followed him into danger and somehow they had won through. They had protected each other, had suffered setbacks and kept fighting. They were his family now, and they'd find a way to help him.

It was his last thought before the pain overwhelmed him and he slipped into unconsciousness.

REALMS ARCANA

PART TWO

THE MORTAL REALMS

Each of the Mortal Realms is a world
unto itself, steeped in powerful magic.
Seemingly infinite in size, they contain
limitless possibilities for discovery and
adventure: floating cities and enchanted
woodlands, noble beings and dread
beasts beyond imagination. But in every
corner of every realm, a war rages
between the armies of Order and the
forces of Chaos. This centuries-long
conflict must be won if the realms are
to live in peace and freedom.

AZYR

The Realm of Heavens, where the immortal King Sigmar reigns unchallenged.

AQSHY

The Realm of Fire, a region of mighty volcanoes, molten seas and flaming-hot tempers.

GHYRAN

The Realm of Life, where flourishing forests teem with creatures beyond counting.

CHAMON

The Realm of Metal, where rivers of mercury flow through canyons of steel.

SHYISH

The Realm of Death, a lifeless land where spirits drift through silent, shaded tombs.

GHUR

The Realm of Beasts, where living monstrosities battle for dominance.

HYSH

The Realm of Light, where knowledge and wisdom are prized above all.

ULGU

The Realm of Shadows, a domain of darkness where dread phantoms lurk.

SKAVEN MAGIC

Though their greatest strength lies in their continually growing population numbers, the cruel and cunning ratmen known as the Skaven also utilise powerful warlocks to achieve their goals. Some Skaven use their magic to spread disease and pestilence, others to create mystical weapons to use against their enemies. But all the Skaven clans make use of gnawholes, mystical portals torn in the fabric of space that allow the Skaven to wreak havoc across the Mortal Realms.

SKAVEN WARRENS

The Skaven dwell in vast warrens of earth and stone, uncharted labyrinths consisting of endless tunnels and gigantic cave systems. However, these warrens do not always obey the same physical laws as human habitations: using the same magic as they do to create gnawholes, Skaven warlocks are able to create warrens that exist outside of the eight Mortal Realms, making them all but inaccessible to non-Skaven. Each warren is ruled by a powerful Skaven clan, headed in most cases by a packlord who exerts absolute power over his underlings.

THE LIGHT OF TECLIS

The Light of Teclis
is one of the few
magical artefacts
in existence capable
of opening a gnawhole
to non-Skaven. Created by
the sorcerer Accore and his followers
during a particularly savage series
of Skaven raids against the citizens
of Hysh, the Realm of Light, the device
helped turn the tide against
the ratmen. But during the ravages
that followed, the Lights were
scattered, making their way to different
realms, highly prized by mystics and
scholars – and of course by the Skaven
themselves, who have seized and
destroyed most existing examples.

ELIO

Bearing the mark of Ghyran, the
Realm of Life, thirteen-year-old Elio

is a born healer. His knowledge of potions and cures is second to none, and he's often to be found with his nose in a giant book of herblore. But he's  not just interested in plants: Elio has a keen fascination with all things living, from the tiniest biting insect to the mightiest man-eating manticore. He may not be the realms' greatest fighter, but Elio is clever, thoughtful and considerate.

ELIAS STONEHAND, LORD OF LIFESTONE

The Lords of Lifestone have ruled the city for generations beyond counting. The current lord is named Elias Stonehand – a stout, forceful man fiercely dedicated to the wellbeing of his people. It was Elias's bad luck to assume the lordship during a time of change: Lifestone is no longer the great

city it once was, and he is increasingly
convinced that dark forces are plotting
against his people. But he also has
problems closer to home: Elias and his
son Elio have always struggled to find
common ground, and Elio's growing
friendship with the mysterious Vertigan
has driven them further apart.

KREECH

Bold, devious and
cruel beyond measure,
Kreech is the packlord
of Clan Quickfang, an
increasingly powerful
Skaven faction. Kreech
is unusual among the
Skaven in that he has a
fascination with humans,
or 'man-things', and
particularly their ability to create and
think imaginatively. Kreech sees himself
as superior to his fellow Skaven, able
to control his animal instincts and

act rationally. He has now entered into partnership with an enigmatic noblewoman, who promises power and riches if Kreech will help her achieve her mysterious goals.

WARPSTONE

Warpstone is crystallised Chaos, and perhaps the most highly desired magical substance in all the Mortal Realms. It is particularly sought after by the Skaven, who use it for countless foul practices: employing its mutating properties against their enemies and using its inherent magic to power their weapons. To the ratmen, warpstone is a symbol of privilege, power and wealth, and their thirst for it is unquenchable.

SCRATCH

Bearing the mark of Ghur, the Realm of Beasts, twelve-year-old Scratch's true name and background are unknown. For some time he's been the pet and plaything of Kreech, a mean-spirited Skaven packlord who has kept the boy alive for devious reasons of his own. Scratch has lived underground in Kreech's warren, fashioning clothes to make himself resemble the ratlord he both fears and admires: his hood has ears and he paints whiskers on his face with water and mud. He may have lost the ability to speak like a human, but Scratch is a sly, sharp-witted child, as cunning as any Skaven.

DEEPEARTH DELVERS

Known in some realms as a
Burrowing Blackpelt, the Deepearth
Delver is highly prized by the Skaven
for its thick, soft, ebony-coloured fur.
A distant relation to the common
mole, the delver is many times larger,
weighing as much as ten horses.
It is almost entirely blind, with a
distinctive tentacled nose used for
smelling, and also for sensing buried
shards of warpstone, which the
creature craves. The delver can be
aggressive when cornered, particularly
when protecting its young or its stash
of warpstone.

ABOUT THE AUTHOR

Tom Huddleston is an author and freelance film journalist based in East London. His first novel, future-medieval fantasy *The Waking World*, was published in 2013. He's since penned three instalments in the official *Star Wars: Adventures in Wild Space* series and is also the writer of the *Warhammer Adventures: Realm Quest* series. Find him online at www.tomhuddleston.co.uk.

ABOUT THE ARTISTS

Magnus Norén is a freelance illustrator and concept artist living in Sweden. His favourite subjects are fantasy and mythology, and when he isn't drawing or painting, he likes to read, watch movies and play computer games with his girlfriend.

Cole Marchetti is an illustrator and concept artist from California. When he isn't sitting in front of the computer, he enjoys hiking and plein air painting. Warhammer Adventures is his first project working with Games Workshop.

An Extract from book three
Forest of the Ancients
by Tom Huddleston
(out August 2019)

'We should go to his father,' Kiri said,
breaking the silence. 'We should ask
him for help.'

'I think Lord Elias might be a bit
busy,' Kaspar said, gesturing down
through the coloured glass. In the
valley beyond the city wall spectral
lights blazed, surrounded by legions of
shadowy figures.

'What do they want?' Thanis
wondered out loud. 'And why aren't
they attacking? Look at those ladders,
those siege engines. They could scale

the walls any time they wanted. It's not like the Lifestone Defenders could do anything about it.'

'That's exactly why we should find Lord Elias now,' Kiri argued. 'Before things get even worse.'

'But Elio told us not to,' Alish protested, squeezing the boy's hand. 'He said they haven't spoken in ages.'

'This is more important than some family squabble,' Kiri insisted. 'The lord will have money, and he'll know the best healers.'

'But there are no good healers left in Lifestone,' Thanis argued. 'They all went away when... when everything changed.'

None of them knew what had happened to the city in which they lived. In recent decades it had gone from a thriving place of learning and healing to a half-deserted ruin. The only one who might have known was their master Vertigan, but he'd been kidnapped by the Skaven on the orders of a mysterious woman, leaving only his staff behind.

'Thanis is right,' Kaspar said. 'There are some who claim to be medics, but they're just as likely to make him worse. And this isn't some ordinary burn – it's a magical injury.'

'Adila would know what to do,' Thanis told him, remembering the old woman from Bowerhome. But she was gone now, passing away peacefully in her sleep just a few weeks after Thanis and Kaspar left for the Arbour. 'She always said the Aelf-folk were the best healers. Them and the Sylvaneth.'

Kiri looked surprised. 'The walking trees? They're a myth, aren't they?'

'They're real,' Thanis said. 'They're meant to live out beyond the Stonewoods, past the Everlight River. The place the old folks call the Forest of the Ancients. They even used to come to Lifestone, in the times before.'

'But the Sylvaneth don't help

humans,' Kaspar said. 'Remember the story Marlo used to love, about the foolish thief who hid his gold in the forest, and the Sylvaneth turned him into a tree?'

'But they let his son go,' Thanis reminded him. 'The babe, remember? The tree-folk left him outside the city walls. They were kind because he was so little.'

'Elio's not a baby,' Kiri pointed out. 'And the woods are dangerous, I heard men have disappeared out there.'

'So what are we meant to do?' Thanis asked, a strange certainty building inside her. 'Just sit here and watch him suffer? I mean, I hate trees and nature and all of that stuff. The thought of seeing a Sylvaneth scares me to death. But it's Elio's life we're talking about. He saved us in the warren, now it's our turn to help him.'

'And what about the army camped outside our walls?' Kaspar asked. 'Are we meant to fight our way through?'

Thanis cursed. She hadn't thought of that.

'I, um...' Alish said nervously. 'I might have a way we can get out of the city.' And she lowered her gaze down into the old library, where a large black shape hung suspended in the shadows.

'Are you joking?' Kaspar asked. 'Please, tell me you're not serious.'

Alish had been working on her flying machine for months, but so far she'd been unable to get it off the ground. It was a huge, unwieldy thing, the patched canvas balloon supporting a wooden gondola festooned with steam-pipes and furnaces.

'I'm this close to making it work,' Alish insisted, holding up her thumb and forefinger. 'Give me one night, and in the morning we'll fly out of here.' She raised her flat hand, swooping it like a bird.

Kiri frowned dubiously. 'You're sure

we wouldn't just crash?'

Alish nodded. 'I'm sure. We can save him, I swear.'

Thanis gritted her teeth. 'I'm in,' she said. 'I trust you, Alish.'

'Me too,' Kiri said. 'But this is a big decision. Not just the airship but the tree-people too. Everyone has to agree, or we don't go.'

They looked at Kaspar, who gave a long, uncertain sigh. 'Well,' he said at last. 'I suppose if we all die horribly there'll be no one left to say I told you so.'

They made Elio comfortable on the floor of the Atheneum, covering him with blankets and stacking pillows beneath his head. His skin was ashen and his breathing was shallow, twisted purple vines snaking from the centre of his burn. Kiri volunteered to watch over him while Alish started work on her flying machine, pipes hissing as she stoked the boiler.

'Watching her won't make it any less terrifying,' Kaspar said, taking Thanis's arm. 'Come on, let's try and get some sleep.'

They wound through the corridors of the Arbour towards their respective sleeping quarters. 'I hope the Scraps are okay,' she said as they turned into the old armoury. 'I promised to check in this week, then all this happened.'

'They'll cope,' Kaspar said. 'Marlo's turning into quite the leader, I hear the Scarlet Shadow tried to recruit him. He turned them down, of course. He's a sharp one.'

'He learned that from his hero,' Thanis said. 'Don't blush, it's true. He loved how you always kept a level head, even when everything was going crazy. I wish I could say the same. But I'm scared, Kaspar. Vertigan's gone, Elio's sick, and our only plan is to get in some crazy flying thing and look for a race of talking trees who'll almost certainly murder us. I even lost my lucky penny, the one that convinced me to come here in the first place.'

Kaspar leaned forward, touching her ear. When he drew back there was a coin shining in his palm. 'It must have been hiding back there all along.'

Thanis laughed. 'Where did you really find it?'

'It fell out of your pocket in the warren. I meant to give it back but I forgot.'

'You're always looking out for me, aren't you?' Thanis asked. 'Whatever happens, you're there.'

'Of course,' Kaspar said. 'And I always will be. One of us falls, the other one catches them. Whatever happens, remember that.'

His face had grown suddenly serious, one hand sliding beneath his robe, touching something at his chest. Thanis saw a string around his neck and wondered – when did Kaspar start wearing a pendant? But then he turned away, and the moment passed.

'See you bright and early,' he said, striding off down the passage.

Thanis watched him go. There was no one she trusted more than Kaspar, he'd saved her neck countless times, and she'd saved his. So why did she feel a sudden chill deep inside, as though something terrible was going to happen?

Because something terrible is going to happen, she reasoned. We're about to be eaten by trees. Sighing, she entered her room and closed the door.

Kiri came at dawn, crouching beside the giant's breastplate that Thanis slept in and shaking her gently. She surfaced slowly from dark dreams of scampering Skaven and tall, murderous shrubs.

'Alish reckons we're ready to fly,' Kiri said, looking round the armoury at the rows of aelvish pikes and duardin hammers, silver swords and wooden longbows, shields painted with a thousand different sigils. Her weapon of choice was a catapult, and she was a superb shot. But she was clad in just a simple tunic so Thanis got to her feet, lifting down a coat of looped leather.

'This should fit you.'

Kiri slipped it over her head. 'It's perfect.'

Thanis's own breastplate was emblazoned with the twin-tailed comet of Sigmar; she strapped it on, along with a pair of giant steel gloves. She flexed her fingers and the metal creaked, but there was no time to oil them now. She grabbed Vertigan's staff and headed for the door.

Then a thought struck her, and she paused. 'Are you going to be the leader now?' she asked Kiri. 'I mean, someone needs to be. Alish is too young and Kaspar's smart but he's reckless, he needs someone to keep

him in line. You got us out of the
Skaven warren. You and Elio.'

Kiri blushed. 'I only just got here.
I shouldn't be telling you all what to
do.'

'But Alish looks up to you,' Thanis
said. 'And if it makes any difference
I'd choose you too, especially for
this. You spent a whole year in the
wilderness. I've never been outside the
city.'

'But you're strong,' Kiri said. 'The
toughest of all of us. Maybe you
should lead.'

Thanis shook her head quickly. 'I'm
okay in a fight, but I really don't like
making decisions.'

Kiri laughed. 'How about the two of
us agree to do everything we can to
keep the others safe?'

Thanis thought about it, then she
nodded. 'It's a deal.'

In the Atheneum the airship hung
on its moorings, suspended above

the cracked stone floor. The gondola
was a wooden oval, the shape
Thanis imagined a boat to be, with
tapered ends and an ashwood railing.
On its prow the stuffed head of a
gryph-hound snarled fiercely, and
inside was a winding network of
cogs and gauges and pipes, steam
gushing up into the patchwork balloon
that hung overhead, attached to the
gondola by a complex series of ropes
and struts. Alish and Kaspar were
helping Elio in – he was awake but
weak, grasping at the rickety rope
ladder.

'Alish says we're going to the forest,'
he told Thanis as she approached. 'Off
on a trip.'

'Um, sure,' she said awkwardly. 'Some
fresh air, you'll feel good as new.'

'I couldn't tell him the truth,' Alish
whispered when he was settled. 'He'd
only try and stop us.'

Kiri nodded. 'If it works he'll be
cured, then we can tell him. If it

doesn't...'

She hoisted her leg over the railing, dropping inside. Thanis followed, trying not to touch anything. 'Now these are the pressure gauges,' Alish said, gesturing to a row of dials attached to small steel tanks. 'They control how high we go, or how low. And this here,' she gestured to a spoked, upright wheel, 'controls the steering paddles, so we can turn.'

'You'll be the one flying it though, right?' Kaspar asked. 'You did build it.'

'Of course,' Alish said. 'I'm just telling you how everything works, in case something happens. Okay, hang on now. I'm going to take her up.'

She strode the length of the gondola, twisting dials and checking gauges as the pipes hissed overhead. It reminded Thanis of someone playing a complicated musical instrument, albeit one that could explode and kill them all if Alish hit the wrong note. The skin of the balloon began to tighten, ropes creaking as they rose into the air. Amazingly, it was working.

Then there was a thunk, and they stopped. Thanis peered up.

'Please don't tell me you forgot about the ceiling.'

Alish laughed. 'Of course not. Here, pull this.'

She handed over a length of rope, smiling encouragingly. Thanis gave a tug and high above them cogs began to whir, machinery grinding deep inside the walls. She saw iron counterweights descending all around the Atheneum, and looking up she saw the dome cracking into segments and folding back like a flower, steel petals opening to the sky. It was a magnificent sight.

'We're flying,' Kiri said as they drifted up, the mooring ropes falling away. 'I don't believe it.'

They rose through the open dome, and Alish grinned. 'Neither do I.'

A shaft of sunlight pierced the

clouds as they rose over the
Arbour, the mountains rising peak
on stony peak behind them. The
city of Lifestone was spread below
like parchment, the streets forming
complex circular patterns. Thanis had
never noticed it before, but the three
main streets seemed to mirror the
shape of a concentric rune with a line
through it – the same one Elio bore,
the mark of Ghyran.

They lifted over the Arbour's wall,
those strange, almost man-like stone
figures standing guard over the palace
and the city below. Alish turned the
wheel and they curved around the
peak of a tower, a pair of bright-eyed
goshawks squawking as they passed.
Thanis could see their nests in the
eyrie, hatchlings gazing in wonder as
the strange ship floated by.

Then she looked past the city walls
to the army beyond, and her heart
tightened. They were like a dark
swarm, filling the valley so densely

that not a scrap of open ground could be seen. Tattered banners rose above siege engines built of blackwood, and ugly trebuchets rose on both sides of the river. But the soldiers themselves were indistinct, a scuttling mass wreathed in shadow.

Suddenly Elio gave a shout, ducking into the gondola. 'My father,' he said, gesturing. 'I really don't think he'd approve of me flying.'

Lord Elias stood on the battlements, the fountain on his armour gleaming in the sun. He shielded his eyes as the strange shape drifted overhead, and Thanis gave a wave. The Lord did not respond.

Then they were above the dark army, and Alish took them higher, soaring towards the clouds. Shouts and catcalls sounded in the valley and Thanis saw arrows arcing through the air. But they were too high to be a target; all the dark legions could do was yell and point.

Then Kiri raised a hand, pointing into the distance. 'What's that? A cloud, or...'

'That's no cloud,' Alish said. 'It's moving too fast.'

'And it's cawing,' Kaspar pointed out. Thanis heard it too, a growing clamour of hoarse cries. She could make out shapes in the dark mass – they were birds, she realised, swarming closer.

Then the ravens were upon them, shrieking and flapping as they dive-bombed the gondola. Their eyes were black and so were their feathers, like scraps of pure darkness given form and a kind of hideous, scratching life. The sun blotted out as they descended, moving in waves around the airship.

One swept close to Thanis, claws outstretched, and she struck out with the staff. The bird let out a strangled squawk and plummeted. Another flapped towards Elio, pecking at his forehead as though drawn to the violet scar. Thanis heard a twang and the raven squawked, dropping to the floor of the gondola. Kiri reloaded her catapult.

Kaspar knelt over the fallen raven, inspecting it with horrified fascination. 'The mark. On the wings, look.'

She peered closer. He was right. The birds weren't entirely black; their wings were patterned with silver, forming a single runic symbol. Kaspar drew back his sleeve, exposing his own birthmark. 'It's the same,' he said. 'The rune of Shyish.'

'The Realm of Death,' Thanis said softly.

Then there was a thud and the airship juddered, steam-pumps grinding. They were losing altitude, drifting down towards the waiting army. She saw faces peering up, red eyes glaring hungrily. Some of the soldiers were very pale and thin, waving swords in their stick-like arms.

Alish reached for the controls. 'One of those birds must have got in the works. I can fix it, I just–'

More ravens swooped in suddenly, angling towards Alish as though they knew what she was trying to do. They pecked and clawed, tangling in her hair, wings flapping at her face. Thanis sprang forward, grabbing a raven in each of her gloved fists and yanking them away, strands of Alish's hair still clutched in their vicious, swiping claws. The birds writhed and screeched but Thanis held them firmly, flinging them over the side of the airship.

Kiri joined her and they formed a defensive wall around Alish as she checked the gauges, banging on the pipes with the flat of her hand, trying to shift the blockage. More of the birds plunged in but Kiri aimed her catapult, taking two of them down in quick succession. Thanis hefted Vertigan's staff, feeling three satisfying collisions as she swung it around, and another two as she brought it back down. Kaspar had grabbed one of the mooring ropes and was swinging it like a whip, striking ravens left and right.

Then Alish gave a victorious shout and the steam-pumps caught, vapour gushing up into the balloon. They rose once more, the ravens peeling away, retreating in a tattered flock.